SAGEBRUSH BRIDES:
Journey Toward Home

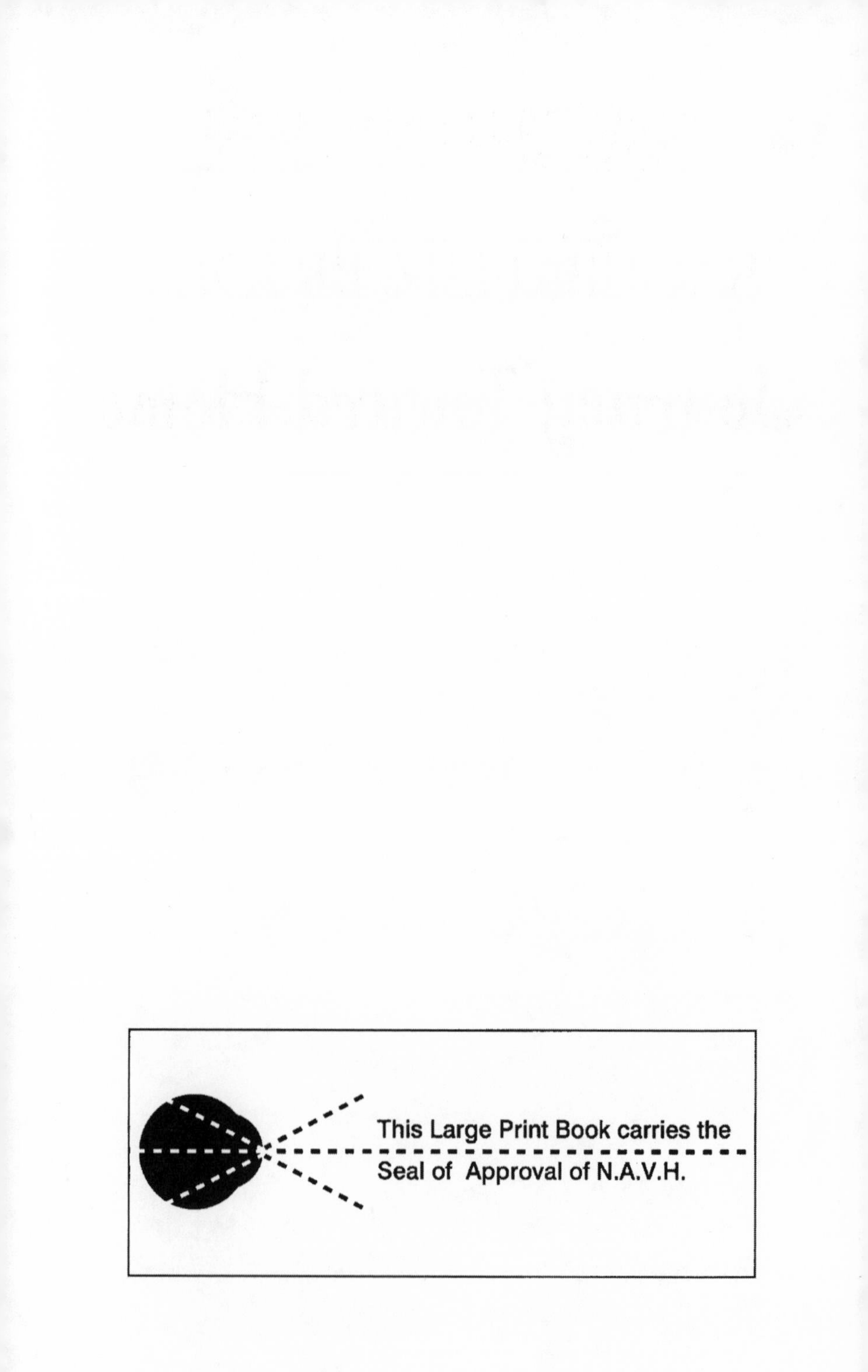
This Large Print Book carries the
Seal of Approval of N.A.V.H.

SAGEBRUSH BRIDES:

Journey Toward Home

Love Rules the Ranch

CAROL COX

Thorndike Press • Waterville, Maine

Sagebrush Brides Collection #1

All Scripture quotations are taken from the King James Version of the Bible.

Published in 2005 by arrangement with Barbour Publishing, Inc.

Thorndike Press® Large Print Christian Romance.

The tree indicium is a trademark of Thorndike Press.

The text of this Large Print edition is unabridged.
Other aspects of the book may vary from the original edition.

Set in 16 pt. Plantin by Liana M. Walker.

Printed in the United States on permanent paper.

Library of Congress Cataloging-in-Publication Data

Cox, Carol.
[Journey toward home]
Sagebrush brides. Journey toward home : love rules the ranch / by Carol Cox.
p. cm. — (Sagebrush brides collection ; 1)
(Thorndike Press large print Christian romance)
Originally published: Journey toward home.
Uhrichsville, Ohio : Barbour Pub., 1998.
ISBN 0-7862-8030-1 (lg. print : hc : alk. paper)
1. Large type books. I. Title. II. Thorndike Press large print Christian romance series.
PS3553.O9148J68 2005
813′.6—dc22 2005018070

SAGEBRUSH BRIDES:

Journey Toward Home

Chapter 1

It was unseasonably warm, and a muggy stillness hung over St. Joseph. I sat in the big wicker rocking chair on Aunt Phoebe's front porch and fanned myself. Aunt Phoebe sat facing me, bolt upright in her chair. Her iron-gray hair, pulled into its customary bun, was drawn so tight that I wondered for the thousandth time how she was able even to blink. She pursed her thin lips.

"You're a foolish, ungrateful child, Judith. How you can disregard the kindness and generosity I've shown you these past ten years, I cannot imagine. Your mother would never have considered doing such a thing. It is obviously the bad blood you inherited from your father."

I clamped my own lips together to keep silent. We had been over this same ground endlessly in the last two weeks. It would be pointless and perhaps fatal to my plans to open another argument and antagonize my aunt further.

Aunt Phoebe had taken my father and me into her home after my mother died in the influenza epidemic when I was ten. At the time it seemed like the most natural thing in the world, given her autocratic personality and the need to "keep a firm hand" on my father, as she put it.

Papa had been a point of contention between us for years. Gentle, fun loving, and idealistic, his was the complete opposite of Aunt Phoebe's pragmatic nature. Her determination to have us share her large house owed more, I believed, to duty than to affection — an attempt, perhaps, to atone for her lapse in allowing her younger sister to marry him.

"I don't mean to seem ungrateful," I said, choosing my words with infinite care. "But in his letter, Uncle Matthew sounded as though he really needed me to come." I didn't mention how much I longed to go.

"Matthew!" She sniffed in contempt. "Your father's brother, through and through. A complete reprobate if ever I saw one! Whatever possessed him to write after all these years of silence, I will never know."

I didn't know what had prompted his

letter, either, but I blessed him for sending it. We never had the opportunity to know one another well. He left for the gold fields in 1859. I remember seeing him off, holding my father's hand and waving frantically at his wagon, lettered on the side with PIKES PEAK OR BUST. He waved back jauntily, his merry voice booming out, "Come and join me when I get settled, Robert. We'll both make our fortunes!"

After that, we received a few sporadic letters, each one from a different gold camp, until finally they stopped coming altogether. Then two weeks ago, another one arrived, a heaven-sent missive addressed to Miss Judith Alder. It read:

Dear Niece,

Word has reached me that my brother, Robert, has been dead these past three years. I am now the proprietor of a trading post near Taos, New Mexico Territory. I can no longer share my good fortune with your father, but if you choose to join me, I can offer you a home and a share of my future profits. I could sure use your help, as I'm a poor hand at housekeeping and worse at dealing with figures. If you de-

cide to come, anyone in Taos can tell you how to reach me.

Your loving uncle,
Matthew

P.S. I cannot pay for your passage at present, but I am sure that in short order we can build a prosperous business.

My heart soared as soon as I finished reading it. There in my hands lay the possibility of escape from dependence on Aunt Phoebe. After opening her home to us, she had never allowed us to forget the debt we owed. I felt gratitude toward her for all she had done, but I yearned to shake off the status of poor relation.

I thought back to my father. He rarely mentioned his brother in his later years, the time that stood out in my memory being during his final battle with the consumption that had claimed him.

"They tell me that a drier climate in the early stages might have helped," he said wistfully. "Perhaps I should have followed Matthew west, after all."

In that moment my mind was made up. I would follow my uncle in my father's stead. All that remained was to convince Aunt Phoebe.

I broached the subject as delicately as I could, but my caution didn't soften Aunt Phoebe's reaction one whit. She alternated between stony stares of disapproval and long tirades in which she took me to task for my ingratitude. I was tempted to answer her sharply, but I held my tongue. I had been left without a cent of my own, and if she refused to help me with the cost of my passage, my adventure would be over before it had begun.

"As I've told you," I said, trying not to let desperation show in my voice, "I promise I'll repay the money for my fare west just as soon as I've earned it in Uncle Matthew's trading post."

Her sharp eyes studied me for a long moment before she spoke. "I have made inquiries and have been informed that it is possible to make a comfortable income from such an enterprise. I am certain, though, that wastrel uncle of yours will squander every dime before you ever lay eyes on it."

I swallowed hard.

"However," she continued, "I can see that you are determined to go." Her eyes misted over. "Just like your mother, you are bent on following the Alder will-o'-the-wisp, probably to your ruin. But, foolish or not, I will not stand in your way."

"Oh, Aunt Phoebe!" I cried.

"Just a moment," she snapped, her eyes once again hard and bright. "You may delude yourself if you choose, but I will not. You say you will repay the cost of your fare. Very well. I accept your intent, although I do not foresee that you will be able to earn enough in your uncle's care to have more than you need just to keep body and soul together. Nevertheless, I am prepared to finance this venture of yours."

She raised her hand before I could interrupt. "But I refuse to throw away any more money than necessary on a fool's errand. I have looked into the various means of transportation to Taos. The railroad and stagecoach would be the fastest methods, but the fare is over two hundred dollars, far more than I am willing to spend."

I looked at her, puzzled. What on earth did she have in mind?

"I have, however, discovered a way that should suit us both." She gave me a wintery smile. "As you know, with the advent of the railroad, most of the travel west by wagon has ceased, at least those wagons starting from Independence. It is my understanding that most of those who still use that method of travel go as far as possible on the train and outfit themselves at the terminus.

"But I would hardly send a young girl, no matter how headstrong, to choose someone suitable to travel with in that rough environment. Therefore, I have made arrangements for you to leave from here by wagon."

My head spun. A trip by covered wagon, taking weeks instead of days? Surely she wasn't serious! But a look at the grim set of her jaw assured me she was.

Well, I considered, *why not?* Uncle Matthew had gone that way himself. It would be arduous, I was sure, but what better way of experiencing the country that was to be my new home than to see it at a slow wagon's pace rather than whizzing by on a train? The more I thought about it, the more enthusiastic I became.

Aunt Phoebe was speaking again. ". . . a family of good character but without funds to make the journey by train. They will leave St. Joseph on Saturday, four days from now. They have agreed to take you along for a nominal fee and for your help in cooking or any other tasks that should arise. If your desire to go trailing off after your uncle is as great as you say, I'm sure you will be willing to employ whatever means necessary to get there."

"I'll do it," I told her without hesitation. "And I will pay you back every penny."

She might have thought this scheme would discourage me, for my quick acceptance seemed to surprise her; she had little to say after that. The days flew by as I made my preparations, considering what to take, what to leave, packing and repacking as I changed my mind. I decided in the end to take little besides my clothing, toilet articles, and my Bible. I would have a roof over my head at journey's end, and surely Uncle Matthew would help me secure anything I might need after my arrival.

My trunk was packed and ready early Saturday morning. Aunt Phoebe refused to go with me to the Parkers' home but did unbend enough to allow Peter, the handyman, to drive me there in the buggy.

At our parting, she surveyed me one last time, said, "When you've seen the folly of your ways, you may come home," and went back into the house.

Peter and I drew up in front of a rundown house on the edge of town. A gaunt woman was supervising the loading of box after box into a covered wagon already laden with tools and furniture. I stepped down, surprised at my nervousness. "Mrs. Parker? I am Judith Alder."

Ignoring my outstretched hand, she said, "Let's see how much extra weight you've brought."

I signaled Peter to carry my trunk to the wagon. "Put it down!" she ordered. "Just as I thought. You've loaded up with so much finery, you won't be leaving any room for us and the things we need."

She hauled an empty box, identical in size and shape to the others being loaded, over to my trunk. "You'll take just as much as you can put in that and no more. These crates will just fit inside the wagon, and I'll not have a big, fancy trunk cluttering things up. I've no doubt you'll all but eat us out of house and home on the trip, but there's no need to start out taking up more than your share of room. We might just as well understand each other from the first." And with that, she went back to bullying the men working at the wagon.

I stared at her retreating figure. So this was the woman of good character Aunt Phoebe had chosen! And we would be spending weeks in each other's company. I groaned inwardly, then squared my shoulders. Life with Aunt Phoebe had increased my immunity to intimidation. I could tolerate a few more weeks of the same if it helped me reach my goal.

Frantically, I transferred as much as I could to the rough box. Some of the clothes would have to be left behind. I picked up my Bible and bag containing my personal items. If I had to, I would carry those myself.

"Are you sure you want to do this, Miss Judith?" Peter frowned, concern in his eyes. "If you want to go back, I can have you home in no time."

I shook my head quickly before my resolve weakened. "Thank you, but no. If you'll just take my trunk back, I'll be grateful." I gave him a smile that was meant to look confident and walked over to the wagon.

Mrs. Parker barely acknowledged my presence beyond nodding her head in my direction and informing her husband that I was "the girl." He looked me over and grunted. Evidently, I had been weighed in the balance and found wanting. A boy who looked to be sixteen or seventeen jumped down lightly from the wagon and wiped his brow on his sleeve.

"I think that's it, Ma." He grinned.

Ma? It was hard to believe this pleasant-looking youth could be the product of the two sullen individuals I had just met.

Seeing me, his grin broadened. "You must be Miss Alder. I'm Lanny Parker. I'm sure glad you're going to go with us. It'll be real good to have company."

The shock of finding a Parker capable of such a lengthy statement rendered me speechless, but I was able to return his smile with enthusiasm. He might be glad of my company, but he had no idea how profoundly grateful I was for his. At least there would be one friendly face along the way.

The boxes were stowed, the mules hitched. Everything appeared to be set for our departure. I looked around, struck by the fact that I was leaving and how little it mattered to me. In my mind, St. Joseph had already ceased to be home.

Mr. Parker mounted to the driver's seat, his wife beside him. I put up my hands to catch hold of the sideboard and pull myself up and over the tailgate.

"What do you think you're doing?" Mrs. Parker's voice rasped. "You and Lanny will walk. We'll spare the mules as much as we can."

Lanny fell in beside me as I walked with my head bowed, trying to hide my mortification. "Don't mind Ma," he said. "She's got a sharp tongue but a good heart."

Well hidden, I thought. But the friendly overture had its effect, and soon I was telling him about Uncle Matthew and my hopes for the future.

Mrs. Parker looked back. "Lanny! Come up here and walk by me."

He gave me an apologetic look and trotted off.

I plodded along by myself, staying off to one side to keep out of the dust. *Think about Taos,* I reminded myself. *Just keep that thought before you for the next few weeks. This won't last forever.*

Days later, I questioned that last thought. We had been on the trail for less than a week, but already it had given me a new perspective on eternity. Day followed day with tedious predictability. We awoke before daybreak, ate, and moved on with as little talk as possible. Mrs. Parker, holding steadfastly to her sullenness no matter how pleasant the circumstances, assigned Lanny and me to opposite sides of the wagon each morning, giving us little opportunity for conversation.

I didn't understand her motive for this until I overheard an exchange between her and her husband on our third morning out. I was busy packing the cooking utensils away inside when they stopped just outside, their voices clearly audible through the canvas.

"I never reckoned on making the girl walk all the way to New Mexico." Mr. Parker sounded troubled. "No reason she can't ride a bit. It'll give us a chance to stretch our legs."

"And who would be driving while she rides? Lanny? Can't you see he's got eyes for nothing else? You're a man. You know where that leads.

"We agreed to take her on," she continued, "but she'll keep to herself on the way. And, mind you, keep your own eyes where they belong!"

I pressed my fist against my mouth to stifle a cry of dismay and sat quietly until they moved away. Angry tears mingled with a desire to laugh. Never before had I been cast in the role of a Jezebel! Couldn't she understand that I only wanted human companionship?

Very well, I would walk every step of the way, if necessary. Only a few weeks to endure this, then I would reach Taos and Uncle Matthew.

Chapter 2

It was a great relief when we arrived at Council Grove and Mr. Parker announced we would be staying there for a day or two.

"There's three other wagons waiting here already and more expected," he said that night over supper. "We'll form a train and have just that much more protection the rest of the way."

The prospect of being around friendly, talking human beings was encouraging. The wagons clustered together a little way outside town on the banks of the Neosho River. Cordial-looking women approached as we cooked supper over our fire, but a few sharp words from Mrs. Parker soon sent them on their way, shaking their heads.

I started to speak, but Mrs. Parker's warning look made me hold my tongue. I gazed after them wistfully. It would have been refreshing to have a good woman-to-woman talk. Maybe things would change once we got under way.

Two more wagons arrived during the next day, and the men from the six groups met together to elect a captain, choosing a self-assured man named Hudson. He had experience with the trail ahead and made the announcement that we would leave the following morning.

I hoped for more interaction with the others of the train — perhaps with women who, like myself, walked much of the time. But the Parkers discouraged contact and kept our wagon well to the rear of the train. So we made our way across the plains with the wagon train, yet not really a part of it.

The sheer size of this land was staggering. For mile upon mile, I saw a billowing sea of green everywhere I looked. The stems of the grasses reached to the horses' bellies, and many of the seed heads grew well above my eye level.

At Cow Creek we stepped out of that world and into another, as though we had crossed an invisible boundary line. Listening to Mr. Parker repeating what he had picked up from Mr. Hudson that day, I learned that we had come to the shortgrass prairie.

The buffalo and grama grasses grew only inches tall, and instead of the waving softness of the tall grass, the land stretched out in a stark panorama as far as the eye could see.

Moving out of the cover of the tall grasses and into the open made me feel more vulnerable. I felt grateful for the protection of the others in our party.

Lanny made things more bearable when he could by talking to me at breakfast and after supper. Once he slipped me a nosegay of wildflowers, still wet with dew. I smiled at him, grateful for his thoughtfulness, and hid the bouquet before his sharp-eyed mother could spy it.

On the first evening past Dodge, we assembled for a meeting. Mrs. Parker, Lanny, and I sat well away from the rest of the group, but Mr. Hudson's voice carried clearly.

"Folks," he said, "we need to take a vote on the direction we follow next. As some of you know, the trail divides a little way from here. We need to make a choice on which fork we take.

"The easiest way, and the one I recommend, is the Mountain Branch. It's about a hundred miles longer, but we follow right along the Arkansas River like we've been doing, and we're sure of water all along the way."

"What's the other fork like?" asked one of the men.

"The other way is the Cimarron Cutoff. It's sometimes called the *Jornada de Muerte* — the Journey of Death." Prickles ran down the back of my neck as he spoke.

"The first fifty miles are without water at all. You'd have to take all your wagons can carry and pray it's enough to last you until you reach the Cimarron."

"What then?"

"The Cimarron's a contrary river. Maybe it'll be running, maybe it won't. The decision is up to all of you, but my advice is to take a little longer and be sure of reaching Santa Fe."

The general murmur of assent reassured me even before the vote was taken that the other men saw the wisdom of his advice.

"All in favor of following the Mountain Branch say 'Aye,' " called Mr. Hudson, and a chorus of "Ayes" rang out. "Anyone in favor of the Cutoff?"

"I am," said a lone voice, and I realized with horror that it belonged to Mr. Parker.

A man standing nearby wheeled and stared at him. "Are you crazy, man? I've heard stories about that stretch. We'd all be risking our lives and our families."

"You heard Hudson. It's a hundred

miles shorter. I'm in a hurry to get where I'm going."

"So are the rest of us. But we want to get there alive."

"All right, then," said Mr. Hudson. "It looks like it's settled. The majority votes to take the Mountain Branch, and I must say I'm relieved. When we come to the fork tomorrow, we'll follow the right-hand branch."

"Not me." The words fell like a heavy stone into the startled silence.

"He can't be serious," I whispered to Mrs. Parker. "We can't undertake a trip like that alone."

"He knows what he's doing," she replied. "We aim to get this over with as quick as we can."

"But she's right, Ma." Lanny looked as worried as I felt. "We get off by ourselves like that and we're in trouble. If we can't find water or we run into outlaws or Indians, we're all alone. There'll be no way to get help."

Mrs. Parker gave him a withering look. "Siding with her against your own parents, are you?"

The men followed Mr. Parker to our wagon, trying to reason with him.

Mr. Hudson grabbed his arm. "Listen to

me, Parker. I've been down the trail before. I know the Cutoff. Why, even the jackrabbits carry three days' rations and a canteen of water out there. Think of your women, if nothing else."

"My mind's made up." Mr. Parker's face was set. "The rest of you do as you like. We're taking the Cutoff."

Sleep did not come easily that night. Fragments of conversation tumbled through my mind. *Fifty miles . . . no water . . . Jornada de Muerte . . . Journey of Death.*

By morning, the rest of the train seemed to have accepted the Parkers' decision, although I saw worried glances cast in our direction more than once. Shortly before we started out, Mr. Hudson came over to our wagon and handed Mr. Parker a sheet of paper.

"If you're bound you're going that way," he said, "at least take this with you." Peering over Mr. Parker's shoulder, I could see he held a crudely drawn map. "I've marked the route the best I could, and I've circled the places where you'll find springs. You'll need 'em, especially if the riverbed's dry."

Mr. Parker thanked him with a grunt, and we waited to hear the order to move out for the last time.

My palms grew sweaty when we reached the point where the trail forked. Five wagons moved on ahead. Ours pulled to a halt and watched while they became smaller and smaller dots on the landscape.

We forded the Arkansas and headed southwest.

We had taken Mr. Hudson's advice and drunk as much as we could hold before leaving the river. The water barrels were filled to overflowing. I breathed a prayer that Mr. Parker knew what he was doing.

The heat was not the only thing against us. Dust, churned up by the wagon wheels and the mules' hooves, billowed into the air in great clouds. When it settled, it blanketed everything — the wagon, the mules, and us. I gave up trying to brush it off my clothes after the first day and concentrated on keeping it out of my eyes and mouth as much as possible. The sight of it constantly swirling about made me even thirstier than before.

Our pace slowed as the heat increased, and by the end of the second day, we were all concerned about whether the water supply would hold out. I sipped my evening ration slowly, savoring every drop.

The mules needed an ample supply to

pull the heavy wagon. I felt sorry for the hollow-eyed creatures, but it was hard to watch Mr. Parker and Lanny pour out the precious liquid for them to drink. Mrs. Parker evidently felt the same way about me, for I saw her jealously eyeing every drop I swallowed.

Late in the afternoon of the third day, Lanny spotted trees on the horizon. We pressed on, bone weary, and eventually reached the banks of the Cimarron.

It was dry.

"Where cottonwoods grow, there's bound to be water," Mr. Parker said and began scooping sand from the riverbed. The sand grew darker as he dug, and finally a chalky white liquid began to ooze into the hole. The mules strained to pull the wagon closer.

Lanny moved a little farther up the riverbed and soon had enough in the hole he scooped out to fill a cup for each of us. It was brackish and back in Missouri would have been scorned as unfit to drink. But it was water nonetheless, and we drank deeply, cup after cup.

In the morning, Mr. Parker consulted the map he had been given. "I figure we're right about here," he said, indicating a spot with his forefinger. "We need to find one of the springs. Looks like the closest one is here." He pointed to a circle on the map.

"How far?" Lanny asked.

"Ten miles. No more."

"Then how far to the next water? And the next?" Mrs. Parker's voice rose shrilly, and I looked at her in amazement. It was the first real emotion that she had shown in all our time on the trail.

"We'll make it," said her husband.

"What about her? She'll use up water the three of us need." She seemed on the verge of hysteria.

"We'll make it," he repeated.

We reached the spring before noon, sooner than we expected. *Now,* I thought, *I understand what an oasis is.*

The water bubbled up, clear and fresh, in the middle of a stand of tall, cool grass. Scattered trees afforded shade from the sun. After blissfully drinking my fill at the spring's edge, I sank down in the grass under spreading branches and felt a light breeze play over my face. I loosened my bonnet strings and let the bonnet slide back on my shoulders so the breeze could stir my hair. It felt wonderful.

The Parkers sprawled around the spring while the mules drank and drank. Relief from the heat and thirst made them seem almost companionable.

We sat like that for a while, enjoying the breeze, the shade, and the freshness of the grass. I hoped we would camp here for the night, but after a time, Mr. Parker got to his feet and nodded at Lanny.

"Give me a hand with the water barrels. We've got to fill up and keep moving."

"Now, Pa?" Lanny's plaintive tone echoed my sentiments. "We're just beginning to cool off a little."

"Get a move on, boy. Your mother and I know what we're doing." Lanny groaned but rose to obey.

I sighed. At least we would have fresh water for the next leg of the journey. I jumped when I realized Mrs. Parker was standing beside me. I hadn't heard her approach.

"Mr. Parker and I have been talking," she said abruptly. "We're all tired and covered with this awful dust. Would you like a chance to wash here before we go on? We can pull the wagon over beyond those trees so you'll have some privacy."

I could hardly believe my ears, but she looked as though she sincerely wanted me to agree.

"Why . . . thank you. I'd like that very much." Her unexpected concern touched me. Perhaps she wanted to make amends for her earlier attitude.

No matter, I thought, as the hoofbeats of the mules grew fainter and I could no longer hear the creak of the wheels. Whatever the reason, I had the opportunity to get clean, and I intended to make the most of it!

I shook as much dust as I could from the folds of my dress and spread it out on the grass to air a little. I had taken a piece of soap from my bag before the wagon moved away, and I carried it with me as I stepped into the spring.

The cold water closed around my ankles with a delightful shock. It was deeper than I had expected, and I squatted down in the center, enjoying the luxury of washing the caked dust from my arms and shoulders.

I scrubbed and scrubbed until my skin glowed, then undid the pins holding my hair and soaped and rinsed it until it lay clean and shining across my shoulders.

I dried off as best I could, feeling revitalized but somewhat guilty at the amount of time I had spent in the water. Dressing hurriedly, I hastened to the other side of the grove of trees, hoping the Parkers wouldn't be too angry about my prolonged absence.

I needn't have worried.

When I emerged from the screen made by the trees, the Parkers and the wagon were nowhere to be seen.

Chapter 3

I stood facing a vast emptiness, my clothes still sticking in places to my damp skin, and searched vainly for the white canvas wagon cover. Always before on this trip, it could be spotted at a distance, the cloth rippling in the breeze like mighty sails.

Nothing.

They must have gone a little farther ahead. Perhaps they changed their minds and were finding a place to camp nearby, after all. Even as I considered the possibility, my mind rejected it.

What if the Parkers had fallen asleep, and the mules wandered off? If they woke up to find the wagon gone, they might even now be trying to catch up to it. We had entered rougher terrain; the landscape might look flat at a distance, but it held an amazing number of rises and depressions. It would be possible, in this broken land, for a whole wagon train to travel along the bottom of a draw and remain all but invisible save to one at a higher elevation. Yes, it was possible they were only hidden from my sight, in one of the distant ravines.

But the head start needed would surely be greater than any distance covered by an aimlessly wandering mule. I fought down a rising sense of panic and began to follow the wagon tracks.

My legs wanted to betray me at every step and break into a headlong run, but I fought the feeling. Had I begun to run wildly as I wished, the panic would have overtaken both my body and my reason in short order. I forced myself to walk along the track deliberately and to marshal my thoughts.

I half expected the wagon tracks to wind deviously to some place of concealment, but to my surprise, they continued openly along the trail. The wagon itself, though, was nowhere to be seen. Not even a cloud of dust marred the western sky.

An idea tried to creep into my mind, and I made every effort to subdue it. The very thought was enough to give me a chill, even in the noonday heat. But it teased and pulled at the edges of consciousness until it made its way to the center of my thinking and had to be faced head-on: I had been deliberately left behind.

The full implications of that did not strike me all at once, which was a mercy. My first feelings were of disbelief and outrage. I was hardly a piece of excess baggage to be cast aside when its burden became too great to bear! I felt ready to march into the nearest town, tell the local constable what had happened, and demand that he take action. So great was my wrath that I actually took several steps down the trail before I came to myself and realized that the nearest town was a good many miles away.

I stumbled to a halt, knocking one foot against an object I had not previously noticed in my anger. It took a moment to gather my senses and realize what sat before me.

It was my box of belongings. In a last uncharacteristic act of charity — or was it merely to drop surplus weight? — the Parkers had stopped their wagon to leave the pitifully few items I brought with me. My Bible lay on top, along with the bag containing my small personal effects.

The enormity of my situation hit me then, and my knees gave way, dropping me down next to my box. I truly had been left, and I faced whatever perils might come upon me quite alone. Incidents along the journey came to mind — comments and complaints about the amount of space my belongings and I took up, the quantity of food and water consumed, and particularly Lanny's supposed infatuation with me. In Mrs. Parker's mind, I was merely an excess piece of baggage and a potentially dangerous one at that.

I recalled her kindness to me, her suggestion that I might like to bathe. Once I had been disposed of, it would have taken them little time to put enough distance between us so that there was no possibility of my overtaking them.

The crate puzzled me. Perhaps a twinge of conscience prompted them to set it by the trail, where it presumably would be found. On a less charitable note, it also gave Mrs. Parker more room to arrange her own belongings.

At least I had my Bible. I reached for it with a hand that trembled and opened it on my lap. A light breeze fluttered the pages. The underlined words in Proverbs, chapter three, caught my attention: "Trust in the Lord with all thine heart; and lean not unto thine own understanding. In all thy ways acknowledge him, and he shall direct thy paths."

Papa always stressed the importance of

applying the truths of the Scriptures to daily living. "Do not read God's Word merely for the pride of having read it, Judith. Head knowledge without heart knowledge is an empty thing." If ever I needed my path directed, this must surely qualify as an applicable time.

I stood up and gazed as far as my eyes could see in either direction. With the sun nearly overhead, east and west looked much the same. For a few panic-stricken moments, I couldn't tell the difference in direction, didn't know which way would take me back to St. Joseph and which would lead me, eventually, to Uncle Matthew. Reason reasserted itself, and I reminded myself that if I waited a short time, the new position of the sun would point me westward.

Nothing in my life up to this point had prepared me for any such turn of events. As far as I could tell, only two courses were open to me: I could give way to my feelings, fling myself down upon the trail beside my belongings, and weep with abandon, or I could choose to travel either east or west and proceed steadily and rationally in the chosen direction.

The first alternative seemed by far the more tempting, especially as the shock bore down upon me. But I realized that would only exhaust me and leave me prey to any danger that might arise.

Traveling alone, on foot, and helpless was hardly a thing to be desired, but I determined that even if the end should come soon, as seemed all too likely, it would not find me groveling mindlessly.

Not knowing how long this frame of mind would last, I turned to open my crate before my resolve faltered to see which belongings might reasonably be carried along with me.

I pried up the lid and stared in disbelief. Even in their one act of thoughtfulness, the Parkers managed to leave me high and dry. The clothes in the crate were not mine but Lanny's.

I sank to my knees beside the crate. How — *why* — could they have done such a thing? Perhaps it was foolish, but somehow not having even the meager consolation of my own belongings seemed the crowning blow.

I remembered then how, after my morning devotions, I had set my Bible down with my bag on the crate closest to me. I groaned. Mrs. Parker and her look-alike boxes! Being in a hurry, they would have connected my Bible with my box and dumped it all together.

Now what? Pillowing my head on my arms on the edge of the crate, I felt my hair brush against my face. I had left it loose to dry. My hands reached mechanically to smooth it into a coil at the base of my neck, and I fumbled in my pocket for my hairpins to make myself presentable.

A sudden shock ran through me. Suppose some other traveler happened along. What kind of woman would they take me for? What sort of woman would be put off a wagon in the middle of nowhere? I could think of only one, and the very thought made me blush.

I had envisioned a possible encounter with kindly people, other emigrants perhaps, who would sympathize with my plight, take me aboard their wagon, and see me safely to Taos. But now — the more I thought over my story, the more unlikely it sounded. If it appeared so even to me, how could I hope to convince others that I was indeed an upright, respectable young lady? And failing to convince them, what would be the dangers of being a woman alone in this wilderness?

Snatches of stories I had heard and put out of my mind came back to haunt me — stories of outlaws, coarse frontiersmen, and rampaging Indians. To be sure, the Indians were supposed to have calmed down, and Uncle Matthew had reported no trouble at his trading post, but mightn't there be renegade bands roaming the plains?

I suppressed a shudder and glanced over my shoulder, half expecting to see dark, hostile eyes peering over a rise.

When loose, my hair rippled over my shoulders, a golden cascade gleaming in the sunlight. It was by far my most attractive feature, and I brushed it faithfully one hundred strokes each night. Now my waist-length tresses seemed nothing but a liability.

Wouldn't such long golden hair be prized as a scalp to hang from a savage's lance? Tears of self-pity stung my eyes. It was all so unfair! Abandoned here through no fault of my own, left to the mercy of hoodlums and renegades far from any form of civilization. I scrubbed at my eyes with the back of my hand.

If I were a man, I thought, *I wouldn't be so lost.* Men always seemed to know what to do. Men carried guns to use for protection. A man alone could travel with relative safety. A man . . .

The idea came with startling clarity, fascinating and repulsive at the same time. It was possible, barely, but surely not dignified. On the other hand, how much dignity was attached to becoming an addition to a warrior's scalp collection?

My mind whirled, and I reached into Lanny's box, sorting through the clothes there. Two pairs of sturdy pants lay on top, followed by three shirts, a pair of overalls, socks, and a suit of long underwear. I laid the pants, overalls, socks, and shirts out on the ground; I saw no need to get involved with a man's undergarments.

There were certainly possibilities. Lanny was stockier and taller than I, but with some adjustments, it just might work. I selected the overalls and the cleanest shirt and made my way back behind the trees.

Some time later, a boy stepped out carrying a neatly folded parcel of ladies' clothing. The clothes had not proved to be such a bad fit after all. Granted, the heavy overalls bagged about me, and the cuffs were rolled up to keep them from dragging in the dirt, but that seemed to conceal, rather than emphasize, my figure.

Years before, my father had dressed me in a pair of boy's overalls and smuggled me out to a pasture for a clandestine riding lesson. Sitting astride, he said, was the only sensible way to ride a horse, and his daughter was going to experience that at least once in her life. It was one of many things that would have scandalized Aunt Phoebe, and it was understood without a word being said that neither of us would mention it to anyone.

I remember shrieking with delight while the horse cantered around the pasture. I was able to cling to the mare like a burr and felt that nothing she could do would dislodge me. Overalls or dresses, it made little difference to me in those days. How differently I felt now! Camouflaged or not, I felt undressed and indecent. I nearly changed my mind right then and decided to take my chances dressed as a woman.

Finally, I decided upon a compromise — I would use my new identity only as a protective measure. If I met up with ruffians or hostiles, I would keep quiet, letting my disguise speak for me. If, as I hoped, some kindly people passed by and offered to take me with them, I would — if I judged them upright people — disclose myself rather than accept their hospitality under false pretenses.

This decided, I squared my shoulders and prepared to make the best of a bad situation. My hair caused me concern. I debated the wisdom of cutting it off short and was in the act of rummaging through the lower layers of Lanny's crate for some sharp implement when, to my delight, I unearthed not only a hat but a sturdy pair of shoes as well.

I coiled my hair high on my head, pinned it in place as well as I could, and with the hat jammed down over my ears, fancied I could go on my way with little fear of discovery. The shoes were rather large, but strips torn from one of Lanny's shirts and stuffed into the toes made it possible for me to walk without stepping out of them.

I fashioned a sling out of the remainder of the torn shirt, folded my small bag and Bible inside, and fastened it inside the baggy overalls. Then taking a deep breath, I resolutely turned my face toward the west.

Chapter 4

By sundown of that day, my brave resolve had shattered into a million hopeless pieces. Never before had I felt such utter despair. I had no idea how far I had come or how far I had yet to go. The long drink I took at the spring before leaving hadn't quenched my thirst for long on the dusty trail. And the oversized shoes had rubbed my feet to a raw, painful mess.

How far did Mr. Parker say we had to go until we reached the next spring? Ten miles? But I had no idea how near the trail it might be. I tried not to think what it would mean if I had already passed it.

Doggedly, I planted one foot more or less firmly in front of the other. Even in my exhausted state, I held fast to the knowledge that the only way to be rescued was to keep moving. The setting sun dazzled my eyes, and I stumbled over a stone.

The fall took every last bit of reserve I had. I pushed myself up on my elbows and tried to gather my knees under me. But my strength was spent, and I pitched forward into sweet oblivion.

The next thought to enter my consciousness was that some large dogs had found me and were sniffing my inert form. I waved an arm feebly, trying to shoo them away, and my hand encountered an enormous wet muzzle. Calculating the size of the beast from the dimensions of its nose, I knew it must be monstrous.

The realization jolted me into a sitting position. The sky had darkened, and I could just make out huge shapes milling about me, making snuffling sounds.

I rose cautiously. Fright drove all power of speech from me, and I began backing away from the creatures, but they followed me, sniffing ominously.

Hunger, thirst, fatigue, and the sheer terror of being alone to face this peril nearly drove away my reason altogether.

"Never give way to panic." How many times had I heard my father say that? "Panic will keep you from thinking clearly, and clear thinking is the best weapon you have in a dangerous situation."

I tried to think as I shuffled backward, wincing as the rough boots rubbed my blistered feet. I had no gun, no knife, not even a stout stick to use as a weapon; I couldn't keep the beasts at bay much longer. I was dimly aware of the blood pulsing in my throat, throbbing in my temples. The throbbing increased to an audible pounding, vibrating through the sand at my feet.

It was several moments before I recognized the sound as the galloping of horses' hooves and a potential rescue. No sooner did that recognition strike me than I had wheeled and was staggering toward the sound with all the strength I had left. Darkness was closing in, and I stumbled over the shadowy ground. The thought that I might come this close to rescue and miss it was too great to be borne.

My throat was so parched from thirst that I was unable to scream. I swallowed painfully two or three times and managed a hoarse cry. Hoofbeats clattered nearer, and a black shape drew up almost on top of me.

"Lookee here!" cried a gravelly voice. I sensed, rather than saw, a figure dismount and step close to me. However, I could pinpoint the location accurately due to the overpowering aroma of tobacco and perspiration.

"Over here, boys!" my rescuer shouted,

his breath nearly bowling me over. He fumbled for a moment, then struck a match and held it toward my face. The sudden light hurt my eyes, and I threw a hand up to cover them, stepping backward as I did so.

"Aw, now, if it ain't a kid. Don't be scared, son. You'll be all right. What happened? You wander off from your folks?"

I was saved from answering by a clatter of hoofbeats as two more riders drew up.

"Found 'em, did you, Jake?" asked one.

"Them and something extra. Look here."

"Where?" spoke yet another disembodied voice.

"Right under your ugly nose," said my protector. "It's a kid. A poor, lost kid."

The moon rose as if on cue, brightening the scene enough to reveal three rough, unshaven men, all staring at me.

"Now don't be scared, sonny," said the one called Jake. "We're not going to hurt you. You just tell us where your folks are, and we'll see you get back first thing in the morning."

I opened my lips to speak but could only manage a croak.

"Jake, where's your sense?" said one of

the mounted men. "Can't you see the kid's dyin' of thirst?"

Jake hurriedly untied a canteen from his saddle, mumbling under his breath. The water tasted as sweet to me as it must have to the children of Israel at Elim. I sipped slowly, letting it trickle down my parched throat, and felt its restoring coolness spread throughout my body.

I used the few moments' respite to compose my thoughts. My original plan, to disclose my identity as soon as I was rescued, did not seem wise at this point.

True, the three men seemed inclined toward kindliness, but they believed me to be a young boy with family nearby. What they might feel about a young woman whose only family was hundreds of miles away might be another matter entirely.

Evidently my disguise was working in the moonlight. But I had no way of knowing how well it would conceal my identity when day came. In the meantime, I decided, I would adopt a cautious policy. I would not deliberately mislead these men by my answers, but neither would I volunteer information unnecessarily, at least not until I was more sure of the type of men they were.

I swallowed again. My voice came out in

a raspy whisper. "My parents are dead. I was traveling with another family to go live with my uncle Matthew, but they left me back down the trail."

"*Left* you?" Even by the light of the moon, amazement was plainly written on Jake's countenance. "You mean they just hauled off and left you in the middle of nowhere?"

It was a difficult question. In my new role, I could hardly say that Mrs. Parker had considered me a threat to her son's virtue.

"I guess I ate more than they liked." That much was surely true. I was saved from closer questioning by a snort from one of the other men.

"Leave the kid alone, Jake. Can't you see he's tuckered out? We'll talk to the boss in the morning and figure out what to do with him. Come on, you take him up behind you. Shorty and I can push these strays back to camp."

Jake spat — tobacco juice, I believed — and mounted before turning to me again. "Come on, kid, climb up here. Those two should just about be able to handle half a dozen steers by themselves."

For the first time since hearing the hoofbeats, I remembered the threatening creatures. Now I saw them standing not many yards distant, long, curving horns clearly outlined in the moonlight.

"Steers," I croaked. "Why, I thought they were some kind of huge dogs." Whatever else I might have said was drowned out by wild roars of laughter, which threatened to unseat all three men. Shorty fairly howled, leaning forward almost double and pounding one fist against his leg.

I could feel an embarrassed flush rise from my neck and wash over my face and was doubly grateful for the darkness. Mutely, I accepted the hand Jake extended between guffaws and scrambled up behind him with as much dignity as I could muster.

As the horse carried us away at a trot, the whoops continued but grew fainter. Jake's shoulders convulsed from time to time, although he at least tried to subdue his mirth.

The day's events had taken their toll, and I found myself struggling to stay awake and upright. Eventually, I managed to balance myself so that I could fall into a light doze without danger of slipping off the horse. I had not asked where we were going or how long the trip would be; I was simply too tired to care. Tomorrow could take care of itself.

At some point we stopped and there were other voices. Hands lifted me from the horse and carried me to a blanket roll beneath a wagon. The last thing I remembered was pulling my hat down securely with both hands.

Morning was heralded by the rattle of tin plates, the creak of saddle leather, and a general flurry about the camp. These things penetrated my consciousness despite my exhaustion, but I wasn't brought fully awake until a pair of feet flying past the wagon kicked a shower of dirt into my face.

I raised my head and looked about wildly, trying to remember where I was. No one had taken notice of me yet, so I lay peering into the hazy light of false dawn, trying to take stock of my surroundings.

As my field of vision was limited, the closest things I could make out were occasional pairs of boots striding by the wagon. Farther out, other objects began to take shape in the brightening sky. A large group of horses stood off to one side; some were being saddled, others rubbed down. Farther along to my right was a vast herd of the cattle that had frightened me so the night before. Evidently the men who had found me were part of one of the cattle drives I had heard about.

A sudden chill crept over me. Did women come along on these drives? I was fairly sure they did not. In that case, I must be the only female among all these rough-looking men and with no idea how long they would travel until journey's end.

Cautiously, I rolled to my left side, remembering to make sure my hat was pulled firmly in place. I tucked a few stray hairs back up under the crown and peered out. A group of men sat cross-legged in a circle not ten yards away. Most were wolfing down the contents of the tin plates on their laps, while a few slurped their coffee.

Coffee! The aroma made my stomach double up in a hard knot. I had been so tired the night before that even hunger had not kept me awake. But now I was ravenous.

How should I make my presence known? I recognized none of the men whose faces I could see, and I shrank from revealing myself before strangers. Furthermore, my male garb had proven effective last night, but just how much could I rely on it in the light of day?

I was saved from further speculation by

Jake, whose head suddenly appeared beneath the wagon's floorboards.

"Well, so you've come around, have you?" The kindness in his eyes belied his attempt to make his voice sound gruff. I nodded and tried to shrink back into the shadows.

"I never saw anyone before who could sleep through Cookie's 'Come and get it.' And right under the chuck wagon, too."

"Jake!" called a stentorian voice. "Is that boy still asleep?"

"No, boss," returned Jake over his shoulder. "He's awake and rarin' to go."

"See that he eats before we pull out. He's probably half-starved." As if in agreement, my stomach gave a loud rumble.

"Look, boy," said Jake, his attention focused on me again, "you roll right out the far side of this wagon. There's some water there and soap. And after you've scrubbed off some of the trail dust, you come over and get something to eat."

I moved to follow his instructions but found I had to grasp the wagon wheel to pull myself upright. I could feel the sores on my feet breaking open again.

A basin of water stood on a small shelf jutting out from the side of the wagon. A bar of soap lay beside it, and a grimy towel hung from a nail.

The soap and water felt heavenly, and I wished that I could use them more extensively. My face stung as I dried it on the rough towel. I noticed a small mirror propped up on the shelf and looked in it to prepare myself for the inspection ahead. I gasped in surprise. If Aunt Phoebe had walked past me on the streets of St. Joseph, she would have gathered her skirts about her and gone by without a second glance.

No wonder the towel had made my face sting. Lanny's hat, while good for disguise, had a much narrower brim than my sunbonnet. My face, with no protection, had been sunburned beyond recognition, and my nose had already started to peel. With the battered hat jammed down on my head, I hardly recognized myself.

The freckles I treated so diligently with lemon and buttermilk were putting in a fresh appearance, and I wrinkled my nose ruefully. That was a mistake. My face felt as though it would split. I could feel heat radiating from it even in the crisp morning air.

Well, I thought, *sore it might be but surely not fatal.* And I looked more like a boy than I ever dreamed possible. If I watched myself closely and guarded my tongue, I believed I would be safe for the time being without resorting to overt deception.

Still feeling almost undressed in my rough shirt and baggy overalls, I squared my shoulders, then settled into a slouch, which I told myself looked more boylike, and hobbled around the wagon.

Most of the men had finished eating and were already busy breaking camp, although the first fingers of sunlight were just reaching over the horizon. Three men still sat around the remains of the campfire sipping coffee. One of them was Jake, who motioned me to sit next to him.

He placed a tin plate heaped with beans and biscuits on my lap. "Here you go. Now just set here and eat your fill. We won't worry you till you've had a chance to fill your belly."

I was so hungry that the familiarity didn't even make me blush. At Aunt Phoebe's, we would have been helping ourselves from chafing dishes arranged on the sideboard. The scrambled eggs would have been fluffy delights, the sausages perfectly brown, the toast a delicate gold. There would have been a selection of jams and marmalade in cut glass bowls, and low-pitched conversation would be heard above the soft clinks of silver touching bone china.

Here, a tin plate had been thrust at me, its cargo of beans a towering brown mass. Biscuits dotted the top and their undersides were already getting soggy. But food had never tasted so good.

The beans swam in some sort of broth, and I used pieces of biscuit to sop up the last of the juices. The biscuits were surprisingly light. I glanced at the dour-faced man putting things to rights around the chuck wagon. If he was, as I assumed, the cook, then it wasn't necessarily true that it took a merry heart to make a good meal. The conglomeration on my plate hardly had visual appeal, but it was delicious.

After I had bolted the meal, my hunger was assuaged sufficiently for me to give some attention to my companions. I eyed the two across the fire from under the brim of my hat.

One was drinking coffee, holding the tin cup in both hands to take full advantage of its warmth. His profile looked vaguely familiar, and I thought he might have been one of Jake's companions of the night before. His youthful movements as he rose to stir the embers of the fire contradicted the age suggested by his weather-beaten face and hands. His eyes, too, were those of a young man and held a glint that promised a sense of mischief.

I turned my attention to the man standing directly across from me. My eyes traveled up a substantial length of denim-clad leg, took in strong, lean hands holding the inevitable cup of coffee, and came to rest on a face seemingly carved of granite. A firm chin jutted out, the mouth set in a determined line above it.

Suddenly, he glanced my way, and his blue eyes looked into mine with an intensity that seemed to bore straight through me. I dropped my eyes and hoped my confusion didn't show. My conscience was pricking me painfully.

I picked up my coffee cup. The steam rose to warm my face as I took my first sip. I gasped and was seized by a fit of coughing. Tears stung my eyes as I tried to catch my breath. I had almost succeeded when Jake began pounding on my back solicitously.

"Are you all right, kid?" he asked, his grizzled face close to mine. I managed to nod and secured my hat, which threatened to fly off under his ministrations.

"Fine," I choked out. Either the coffee or Jake's pounding had made me slightly giddy, and I blinked, trying to clear my vision. "Just fine."

"Coffee's no good to a cowboy 'less it's strong enough to float a horseshoe," drawled the weather-beaten man, rising to his feet.

"You hush, Shorty," snapped Jake. "This young'un's had enough trouble without you making fun."

Shorty drew himself up to his inconsiderable height and stalked off with as much dignity as a bow-legged man could muster.

Jake turned his attention back to me. "Now that you've gotten filled up and woke up, you and the boss here need to talk a bit before we head out." He jerked his head in the direction of the man across the fire. "I'll go see to my horse."

I steeled myself to meet that intense gaze again and rose to my feet to reduce somewhat his advantage in height. Even across the fire, I could see that my head wouldn't quite reach the top of his shoulder.

They were broad shoulders. His height was not the gangly awkwardness of some of the young men I had known at home, all arms and legs and lack of grace. He was well proportioned, and his movements as he set down his cup and turned to study me were smooth and agile. I wished I knew what manner of man lay beneath the exterior.

"What's your name, boy?" he asked.

"Ju—" I caught myself, floundered wildly, and managed to stammer, "Judah." Foolishly, I had been unprepared for the question and came up with the first compromise that entered my head.

"Judah. All right. Don't be frightened, son. We only mean to help." He took a long step over the dying coals to stand at my side and threw a muscular arm around my shoulders.

I caught my breath. There was only kindness in the gesture, but the proximity was unnerving.

"Jake told me how he found you. I know it's tough, being without your folks. Mine have been gone a good many years now, since I was fifteen." His grip on my shoulders tightened as the expression on his face softened. "But we'll see you through till the end of the drive, then see about finding a way to get you to your — uncle's, was it?" I nodded. He gave a final squeeze and released me, much to my relief.

"How–how long will the drive last?"

"Not long. We're three days at most from the ranch."

Three days alone with all these men! Resolutely, I choked down my alarm. This was all the help that was available, and I was powerless to change my situation. I would have to make the best of it.

"Let's get moving. It's time to head out." He seemed to be in a hurry, and I tried to match his pace as he strode toward the horses. He noticed my stiff gait and frowned.

"Your feet are raw from all that walking, aren't they? Well, come along, you'd better ride in the wagon."

I limped along behind him to the chuck wagon, where the cook had made ready for departure with amazing speed.

"Cookie, this is Judah," he announced. "He'll be riding with you today." The heavyset man gave me a sour look and began clearing a space near the wagon's tail. Evidently, I wasn't going to sit next to him on the seat.

But that meant less chance of being questioned, I thought, brightening, and it would give me time to reflect on what my next move should be.

The space cleared, Cookie climbed up to the seat and my benefactor turned to go. "Don't worry, Judah. Cookie's bark is worse than his bite. At least," he said with a sudden twinkle, "I think it is. He hasn't bitten me yet."

I suppressed a smile as I scrambled to my perch and raised my eyes to meet his. "Thank you, Mr. —"

"Jeff will do. Short for Jefferson." With that, he was gone. Moments later a roar of "Move 'em out!" echoed through the camp, and we were off.

Chapter 5

From my cramped seat, I could see the cowboys in position alongside the herd. There was beauty and precision in the way they kept the cattle grouped together, slowing the ones in front who would forge ahead and prodding those who tried to lag behind. From time to time, one of the men would have to veer away from the group in order to head off a stray, and the cooperation between horse and rider was a marvel to watch.

Engrossed in the strange ballet, my spirit soared, and I rejoiced in being a child of the God of creation. My throbbing feet soon claimed my attention, however, and I gingerly eased the boots off. Both feet were terribly swollen, as well as being raw and covered with blisters. I winced as the throbbing increased and wished I had a pail of cold water to bathe them in.

Lacking that, I wriggled around sideways so my feet could rest on sacks of flour and my back was propped against the wagon's side.

When I was reasonably comfortable, I leaned back and felt the weight of my Bible pressing against me. I looked around cautiously. Cookie sat hunched over the reins, as unconcerned as if he had nothing more than beans and flour riding behind him. No one was riding near the rear of the wagon, so I reached inside my overalls and drew out my Bible.

I sighed. At least one thing remained constant in my madly changing world. Hardly a day had gone by in recent years that I hadn't begun with time spent reading God's Word. I turned the well-thumbed pages to Paul's epistle to the Ephesians, where I had marked my place — was it only the day before? — and settled back to read.

Chapter four. Paul talks about the unity of believers, their edification, and speaking the truth in love. I was squirming uncomfortably by the time I reached verse 25: "Wherefore putting away lying, speak every man truth with his neighbour." There was a distinct twinge in the area of my conscience.

I flipped the page, and a verse fairly flew out to meet me: "Stand therefore, having your loins girt about with truth."

The Bible lay open on my lap, but my eyes tried to focus on the sacks of flour, the sideboards of the wagon, anything but the printed page.

Shame swept over me. Deception and falsehood — hardly the path I had committed myself to follow! It had seemed such an innocent thing at first, and the initial goal of protecting myself from marauders had not been a bad one. But now I was becoming more and more enmeshed in the lie I had begun.

The Lord had seen fit to bring me to a point of rescue; could I not then trust Him to provide protection from that point on? Granted, last night's exhaustion had muddled my thinking, but I bitterly regretted not having told Mr. Jefferson the truth this morning.

I resolved I would do so as soon as I saw him. After all, he was the one to whom I had lied directly. This resolution made, I asked forgiveness from the Lord and drifted into an uneasy sleep.

A particularly hard jolt of the wagon woke me. From the sun's position and the heat, I judged it to be about noon. The back of the wagon was stifling. I longed to get out and walk in the fresh air, but my feet were so swollen, I couldn't begin to put the boots back on.

I leaned back and consoled myself with the thought that we would soon stop for the noon meal, and I could take that opportunity to confess to Mr. Jefferson.

The wagon lurched along and my stomach began to complain. "Biscuits and some jerky in the box next to you," said Cookie, without turning his head.

I reached into the box and helped myself. The biscuits, I knew, would be good, but I looked skeptically at the strips of dried meat. I tried nibbling at the end of one. That proved fruitless, and I soon found that the only way to take a bite was to grip a chunk firmly between my back teeth and tear it off.

Chewing it was another matter entirely. It took considerable time for it to soften enough to chew at all. It made for slow eating, but surprisingly it was all the more satisfying for that.

The last of my meal gone, I realized I was thirsty and summoned up my nerve to speak to the dour cook.

"Excuse me, will there be coffee when we stop for lunch?"

"Stop?" He snorted. "You just had your

lunch. There's water in that canteen in front of you."

There was, although it was tepid and stale. But it did quench my thirst. I began to develop an appreciation for the men who sat on horseback without a break. Some of them were digging into bags behind their saddles and pulling out what looked to be more biscuits and jerky.

I was anxious to have my talk with Mr. Jefferson. Once more I addressed the cook's forbidding back. "When will we be stopping?"

He snorted again. It seemed to be his most expressive means of communication. "We will be stopping," he said mockingly, "about an hour before sundown. Boy, if you're in such an all-fired hurry, why don't you hop out and run over to some of them bushes over there?"

I blushed hotly as I realized his meaning. That would be the last time I addressed the man, I vowed. He was exactly the coarse type of person I had been hiding from in the first place.

Hiding. That reminded me of my postponed interview with Mr. Jefferson. Now I would have to wait until sundown! Much as I dreaded it, I wanted the peace of having it over and done with.

The pile of sacks wasn't as comfortable now as it had been earlier. I rearranged them as best I could and found some empty sacks to place under me, where the floorboards were growing harder by the minute. With that accomplished, I stretched out as far as I could in my cramped quarters and resigned myself to riding out the intervening hours.

The prairie grasses rustled softly in the light breeze. Cattle bawled from time to time, their voices interspersed with yips from the cowboys. The wind shifted, and the breeze played lightly inside the wagon, cooling my hot face. My hair was still coiled on top of my head under my hat. Its weight was oppressive, but I didn't dare take the hat off . . . not yet.

We rolled across the vast prairie, a herd of cattle, a dozen rugged men, and me. Despite our large numbers, we were no more than a speck in that wide and empty land. I dozed off and on during the afternoon, lazily tracking the sun's path as it headed down toward the horizon.

Late in the afternoon, one of the men rode up alongside the wagon and spoke to Cookie. "Got a place spotted?"

Cookie nodded. "Bunch of trees up there. Should be water. I'll go on ahead and set up if it looks good." The team picked up speed, and we moved away from the herd.

Apparently there was ample water, for Cookie brought the team to a halt. I was pleased to see that keeping my feet elevated during the day had reduced the swelling, and they were nearly back to their normal size. I tried to slip my socks back on, wincing when they touched the raw places.

Cookie pulled down the tailgate, glanced at my efforts with an impassive face, then reached into a box and tossed me a roll of soft cloth strips. "Bandages," he said.

My feet were still tender when I stepped out of the wagon, although the soft bandages did help a lot. My concern for my feet, however, was dwarfed by the pains that shot through every other part of my body. After a full day of cramped inactivity, my muscles felt as though they had frozen stiff.

Cookie was busy building his fire, but he watched as I staggered around stiff-legged, trying to straighten up. A raspy sound came from his direction, like the wheeze from an organ that has long gone unplayed.

He wheezed again. Why, the man was

laughing! My pleasure in discovering that he was capable of such a thing was dampened by the fact that I was the object of his merriment, but it was an encouraging discovery, all the same.

"Boy," he said when he had regained some control, "why don't you go on over and wash yourself?" I was touched by his concern until he added, "You surely look like you could use it." And began wheezing again.

I found a towel in the wagon and went off, reflecting on the strange humor of cowboys.

I returned feeling much refreshed. I had even been able to unwind my hair and brush through it, and the few minutes' respite from its weight on my head had been wonderful.

"Is there anything I can do to help?" I asked Cookie. It was hardly fair to expect to be waited on when these men had so kindly taken me under their wing.

He looked at me appraisingly. "Why don't you scout around for more wood? We'll need enough to keep it going all night long to keep the coffee hot for the night crew."

I stared. For Cookie, this was being positively chatty. I wondered what had brought about the change while I began to gather firewood.

The exercise helped loosen my stiff muscles, and as long as I walked gingerly, I got along rather well. I was proud of the pile I collected by the time the men had brought the herd up and gathered for supper.

They sprawled around the fire in a variety of attitudes, but none of them displayed the bone-weariness I would have expected after a full day in the saddle. Cookie unbent still further and let me help him dish up the supper. The plates were filled with succulent steaks and the ever-present beans. Coffee that looked strong enough to float any number of horseshoes added its fragrant aroma to the evening air.

I scanned the faces in the group. Mr. Jefferson was not among them. I told myself not to worry. He would surely be in soon.

Taking my own plate, I sat at the edge of the firelight. Some of the men had finished eating and were settling down to talk.

"Good thing Andy got that buffalo yesterday," said one.

"Mm," agreed another around a mouthful of food. "Best steaks we've had the whole trip."

I glanced at the bite on my fork. So this was buffalo and not beef. I took a tentative nibble and found it delicious. There was a lot I had to learn in this new land.

"Anybody seen Jeff?" asked Cookie. "He'd better show up while there's food left."

"He and Jake went to doctor a cow," answered Shorty. "She got a leg tangled pretty bad in some cactus."

So now I would have to wait even longer. I watched idly as Shorty rose and left the circle. He picked up a bedroll and looped his rope around it, then strolled over to a nearby tree. Standing beneath it, he gave the bedroll, rope and all, a toss into the air.

My interest quickened. What new practice of the west was this? The roll fell at his feet, and he threw it again, harder this time. The rope caught around one of the branches about ten feet up and hung in a fork, the bedroll swinging from one side, the end of the rope dangling from the other. I waited to see how he would get the tangle loose, but he walked back to his place in the circle and sat down as if satisfied.

One of the other cowboys shook his head sadly. "Shorty, one of these days, someone's going to dangle a loop over a limb that's meant for you."

Shorty grinned. "No chance, Neil. I'm

as pure as the driven snow."

Neil grunted. None of this exchange made sense to me, but so far, very little had.

"Here you go, boys." It was Cookie, bearing a tray of steaming pies. "Enjoy the apples. They're the last you'll get on this ride."

I helped him cut huge wedges of the pies and serve them to the men. Shorty looked up when I gave his piece to him. "Well, boy," he said, "what do you think about those three thousand head of big dogs we're herding?"

The chuckles around me revealed that my comment had been repeated and apparently enjoyed. I ducked my head in embarrassment and kept on serving.

"His name's Judah," Cookie growled. I turned to look at him in appreciation, and he glared back at me, but this unexpected championship made me feel more protected than I had since Jake left me that morning.

Shorty, however, wasn't one to give up easily. "Judah, is it?" he asked politely. "Well, that's fine. Judah, are you feeling better today?"

I nodded, sitting down to eat my pie. His face betrayed nothing, but I was confused by his sudden interest, embarrassed at being singled out, and altogether suspicious of his motives.

"That boy don't talk much, does he?" he muttered. I glanced up to see him eyeing me speculatively.

"Shorty?" It was Neil. "Do you think we'll have any trouble with skunks like we did back in Texas?"

"Well, now, it all depends," Shorty drawled. I breathed a sigh of relief. His attention had been diverted from me; he didn't so much as flicker an eyelash in my direction.

"It all depends," he repeated. "I surely hope not. I recollect what happened to poor Lem Harris. You all know that story, of course."

"Can't say I've heard it," said a man sitting a few feet from me. "Why don't you tell us all about it?"

"It's a sad and terrible story," Shorty began. "About five years ago, I was on a drive near the Brazos. There were only ten of us, including the cook and the wrangler.

"We'd had trouble all along the way, what with Indians, dry waterholes, and wolves waiting to pick off the stragglers if we gave them half a chance. But the worst problem we had to put up with was the hydrophoby skunks."

I shuddered. Here was another new peril. I listened intently to prepare myself in the event I came across one of the creatures.

"You've all dealt with hydrophoby skunks, haven't you?" Several of the men nodded solemnly. "For such timid critters, they turn mighty mean when the disease takes them. Cunning, too. They're just itching to bite someone, but they know they don't stand a chance when you're up on horseback."

"What do they do?" asked the man near me.

"Why, they wait around a cow camp, like this one here, and hide in the grass until everyone's asleep. Then they come creeping out and check the bedrolls, one by one. And the amazing thing is how they always check the head end."

"Can't you just cover your head and fool 'em?" asked my neighbor.

Shorty shook his head. "I told you, they get mighty cunning. They have some kind of instinct for finding the head. Maybe it's the sound of breathing. But they'll creep up and pull the blankets right back from your face."

I looked around cautiously, trying to

search out the shadows. None of the men seemed particularly concerned, though, and no one took the slightest notice of me.

"Anyway," Shorty resumed his tale, "we'd noticed signs of them hydrophoby skunks for some time, and of course I'd warned all the new men about them. Told them that the only way to keep from getting bit if one comes up to you is to lie perfectly still. You know, they have bad eyesight, and they wait for a body to move so they can take proper aim."

"Tell 'em what happened to Lem," prompted Neil.

Shorty sighed mournfully. "That Lem never was one for listening. One night, we were all layin' in our blankets, when I heard a rustling in the grass. I knew it was some kind of varmint, but it wasn't until it began tugging my blankets away from my face that I saw for sure it was a hydrophoby skunk."

"What did you do?" This from my neighbor.

"Do? Why, I just laid there as still as death, and when he couldn't take a proper aim at me, he moved off to check the others.

"Once he was gone, I kind of eased up on one elbow, and I saw him sizing up old

Lem. Lem hadn't taken my warning to heart, and no sooner did the pulling and the tugging wake him than he started up with a yell.

"That was all the skunk was waiting for. As soon as Lem moved, the skunk spotted his target and jumped him."

"How bad was it?" asked one of the men.

"Bit the end of his nose clean off. Lem was up dancing around, whooping and swearing, and in all the excitement, the hydrophoby skunk moseyed off and we never saw him again. Lem never did look quite right after that. Them hydrophoby skunks are mean — poison mean."

In the silence that followed, I realized I was holding one hand protectively over the lower half of my face.

The cowboys got up, stretched, and one by one started laying out their bedrolls. Shorty stopped next to me and laid a hand on my shoulder. "I already spread your blankets out for you, boy," he said kindly. "You'd best get some sleep."

The fire had burned down and the night air was chilly. I would roll up in my blankets, I decided, and wait for the return of Jake and Mr. Jefferson.

Shorty had thoughtfully spread my blankets next to the chuck wagon, and I welcomed its now-familiar shelter. I tossed and twisted, trying to fit my body to the unrelenting contours of the ground.

Overhead, the sky was an indigo blue, with the lighter clouds scudding across it. The moon had nearly completed its circuit and cast a cheerful glow across our campground. The beauty of God's creation held me spellbound, and it seemed impossible for any but the most friendly creatures to exist in the peaceful setting.

Footsteps sounded on the far side of the fire, and I raised my head to see Jake walk into the circle of light. He looked exhausted. He stood for a moment as if puzzled, then frowned and began pacing around outside the circle of sleepers. "All right, where is it?" he yelled. The cowboys lay undisturbed, apparently sound asleep.

Jake turned away, mumbling, and enlarged his circle. He stopped short under a tree and stared up into its branches. "Hey, Shorty!" he roared. "Can't a body come back all tuckered out after a long day's work without finding someone's gone and strung his bedroll up in a tree?"

The bodies around the fire were suspiciously quiet, but I heard a muffled snort of laughter. Until that moment I had forgotten Shorty's strange behavior. The sight of Jake clambering up the tree to untangle his bedroll might have been funny if I hadn't been so tired myself lately and had a fair idea of how he felt.

A movement behind me claimed my attention. On the opposite side of the chuck wagon, I could see two pairs of boots and hear the murmur of voices.

One I recognized as Cookie's. "About time you got in. You look played out. Here, I saved you a plate. It's cold now."

I strained to hear more. This must be Mr. Jefferson.

"Thanks, Cookie. I am tired." It was undoubtedly his voice. My moment was at hand.

"Cow going to be all right?"

"I think so, as long as infection doesn't set in. We'll do the best we can."

I drew a long breath and offered a prayer for strength. I was in the very act of slipping from beneath the covers when Mr. Jefferson's next words arrested my movement.

"How's Judah? Did he give you any trouble today?"

I froze, straining to hear Cookie's reply. "You know, that boy's really something. I figured he'd be up beside me, wanting to drive and jabbering in my ear all day. But he sat in the back where I put him and hardly said a word."

"Is he rested up from yesterday? He's had a pretty rough time of it, being deserted like that."

"I'll tell you, Jeff, that boy's got spunk. His feet were worn as raw as anything I've ever seen, but he never once complained. I gave him some bandages, and darned if he didn't come offer to help me! Gathered that pile of wood all by himself.

"That boy's game, Jeff. I'll stand by him."

"He must be something special to get you to open up," Mr. Jefferson said, chuckling. "That's more than I've heard you say on the whole drive."

Cookie resorted to his characteristic snort and withdrew into silence. I could see the other pair of boots walk away into the night.

It's said that eavesdroppers seldom hear good of themselves. I wondered how many eavesdroppers heard themselves described in such glowing terms, especially when they knew the praise was undeserved.

I could no more have interrupted that conversation than I could have held the chuck wagon up with one hand. My misery increased — not only had I failed to confess my duplicity, but by my silence I had allowed the two men to form a wholly undeserved opinion of me.

The fire was merely a bed of glowing coals by now. I could not make out Mr. Jefferson's form in the darkness, nor could I call out to him for fear of rousing the camp. My confrontation had been postponed again, at least until breakfast. I rolled up in my blankets, thoroughly disgusted with myself, and went to sleep.

I don't know what startled me awake, but all at once my eyelids flew open and I knew something was wrong. A tug on my blankets told me I was not alone; someone was gently pulling the blankets away from my face.

A confusion of thoughts whirled through my mind in what must have been only a split second. One of the men, perhaps. Should I cry out? But surely none of our number would come meaning me any harm, not with a dozen strong, armed men sleeping only yards away. It must be Mr. Jefferson, or Cookie, or Jake, come to bring me some message. But then why not shake my shoulder? Why this insistent tugging to uncover my face?

Something in my sleep-numbed brain

fought for recognition, something that lay just beyond my grasp.

Of course! I nearly moaned aloud in despair. Shorty's story of the marauding skunks! What did he say to do? Lie perfectly still. That was it. Don't give the poor-sighted brute a chance to take aim.

The blanket inched away from my cheek, my nose, my chin. *Remember Lem Harris,* I warned myself. *Lie still, and it will go away, and you can raise the alarm to warn the others.*

The pulling stopped, although I still felt a vibrating tension on one corner of my blanket, as though the beast were trying to focus on my face, to take aim at my nose. It was almost more than I could bear to lie motionless under its steady, if nearsighted, gaze. The black night hid it well, but I could feel its presence as it waited for a chance to spring.

I heard a sudden rustle, and to my terror, a furry body leapt full into my face. I screamed, fighting wildly against both my attacker and the tangle of blankets that held me.

I screamed again and kicked my way free. I caught hold of a fistful of fur and tore it away from my face. There was a roaring in my ears, and I steadied myself.

This was no time to faint.

Movement stirred among the bedrolls, and someone threw wood on the fire, sending up a shower of sparks followed by a strong flame that lit up the camp area.

Through my panic, I became dimly aware that the roaring in my ears was the sound of the men's laughter — laughter that died away as they stared at me, open-mouthed.

I dropped my eyes before their gaze and became aware of three things. One was the piece of rabbit skin I still clutched in one hand. Another was the rope tied to one corner of my blanket and trailing away toward where the men lay. The third was my hat, lying on the ground.

To pick it up and replace it would have been pointless. My hair had fallen loose during my frantic struggle and now hung down to my waist.

I looked back at the men. They still gaped at me. Only Shorty, absorbed in his hilarity, had failed to notice what had happened. He rocked back and forth, the end of a rope trailing from his hand, whooping and slapping his leg.

"Hear that?" he cried. "Did you hear that? I told you I'd get that boy to talk! I told you —" He broke off, eyes bulging as he finally focused on me.

It was Jake who broke the silence. "My word!" he roared. "He's a girl!"

No one else made a sound. I waited hopefully for the earth to open and swallow me up.

Across the fire, a figure stepped into the circle of light, and I found myself looking straight into Mr. Jefferson's eyes.

Chapter 6

The next day found me rocking along in my seat in the rear of the chuck wagon. My feet were over much of their soreness by now, but my pride felt grievously tender.

The much-delayed talk with Mr. Jefferson had finally taken place the night before. We walked to the edge of the firelight while the cowboys rearranged themselves in their blankets. Not one of them uttered a word following Jake's outburst. Even Shorty remained silent.

We stopped just before the darkness enveloped us. I was grateful for the effort made to have a private conversation and devoutly hoped that we were indeed out of earshot. I was sure that anything that might be overheard would spread through the group like wildfire. From what I had seen thus far, when it came to passing along scraps of information, Aunt Phoebe's sewing circle had nothing on these cowboys.

Mr. Jefferson turned to face me. He said nothing, but his eyes demanded an explanation.

"I meant to talk to you earlier," I faltered. He raised his eyebrows. I took a deep breath and plunged into my story.

"My name is Judith Alder. That's the only thing I lied to you about. I really was traveling west to help my uncle Matthew at his trading post. The family I was traveling with drove off and left me yesterday morning, just as I said."

"Why?"

"We were running low on food and water. They'd be more sure of getting to Santa Fe if they only had three mouths to feed. And Mrs. Parker . . ." I hadn't planned to elaborate on that portion of the story, but I had made up my mind to make a clean breast of things, and I would, despite my embarrassment.

"Mrs. Parker, the woman I came with, felt I was an . . . an unsettling influence on her husband and son."

"I can imagine," he said drily. "You've certainly succeeded in unsettling this camp tonight. And did your Mrs. Parker outfit you before she left?"

"Not intentionally. They set out a crate they thought was mine, but their son's clothes were in it. I felt I would be safer traveling alone if I were, ah, incognito."

"I see. But after Jake found you and brought you in . . . ?"

"Please try to understand," I pleaded. "I was so terribly tired and afraid and confused. I had no idea what sort of men you were, and there weren't any other women around.

"After I'd lied to you about my name, I knew I had to tell you the truth and make it right, but I didn't see you anymore today. And after I got in bed, I heard you come in, but then I heard what you and Cookie were saying about me, and I just couldn't bring myself to do it then.

"And then," I gulped, my emotions getting the upper hand, "when you went away, I decided I'd tell you at breakfast, but Shorty played that horrible trick about the hydrophobia skunk, and . . . and . . ." For the first time since being left, I gave way to tears, and they came in abundance.

I covered my face with my hands to muffle the sobs that shook me. Never had I felt so alone and so ashamed. Not only had I purposely deceived the kind people who had taken me in, but I had failed miserably at following the example of Christ.

Mr. Jefferson shuffled his feet. Apparently he felt as uncomfortable as most men around feminine tears. Wiping my eyes with the backs of my hands, I choked back the sobs and waited for whatever censure was to come.

"You're tired, Ju— Miss Alder. You'd best go get what sleep you can. If we push ourselves, we may be able to make the ranch by sundown tomorrow, and you can have a decent bed." His lips tightened. "And a change of clothes."

"Thank you," I said meekly. He stretched out his arm as if to throw it around my shoulders as he had that morning but drew it back abruptly.

"Go get some rest," he said.

After the evening's turn of events, I expected to lie awake for hours. Instead, I slept dreamlessly, noticing nothing until Cookie's "Come and get it!" roused the camp. I elected to stay close to the wagon to eat the plate of biscuits and beans Cookie silently handed me rather than join the men around the fire.

Now it was nearing noonday, and I helped myself to biscuits and jerky. Cookie made no effort at conversation, but then, no one had spoken a word to me all day. I felt a twinge of self-pity.

You've only yourself to blame, I scolded

myself. I wondered if I would be ostracized like this once we reached the ranch. If the story was passed along to the owners . . . If! How could I doubt its being told, and with suitable embellishments, at that.

But they would have to talk with me long enough to let me know how I could reach Uncle Matthew. I sighed. Being passed from hand to hand was growing tiresome.

Late in the afternoon, one of the men rode up next to Cookie. "Jeff said to tell you we're making better time than we thought. He's scouted on ahead, and he says we ought to be at the ranch in an hour or so."

"Good," Cookie said. "It'll give me a chance to unload in the daylight."

Yes, unload, I thought wearily. *Unload the food, unload the equipment, and unload me.* I pulled out my bag and found my comb, then set to work on the snarls in my hair. If we were getting back into civilized country, I had better make myself presentable. Well, as presentable as possible. I fervently hoped the rancher's wife wouldn't turn out to be another Aunt Phoebe.

At least I could make a reasonably fresh start there, and I would be free of the cowboys' scrutiny, Shorty's practical jokes, and the look in Mr. Jefferson's eyes in which I felt sure I had read disappointment and reproach. Once safe inside the ranch house, I need not see any of them again.

I found a small handkerchief tucked away in my bag, soaked it with water from a canteen, and used it to scrub my face and hands. The trail dust, I knew, would settle and cling again almost as soon as I had washed it off, but it boosted my morale to make the effort.

Little could be done about my clothes. I slapped dust from the overalls with my hat as I had seen the men do. Thank goodness I wouldn't have to wear it again! I smoothed my hair as best I could into a coil at the back of my neck, thinking how good it would feel to have it clean once more.

The wagon rocked more slowly now. I tried to peer out the front but could see nothing beyond Cookie's broad back. He seemed determined to maintain his cold-shoulder treatment to the end. I had tried to apologize earlier, but he had gone about his business as though I were not even there.

Cookie drew the team to a stop and jumped off the seat, not bothering to glance back at me. I was sorry to part company on such a cool note.

Jake's face appeared at the back of the wagon. "Miss Judith, we're at the Double B now. Come on out and I'll take you to meet the Bradleys."

He helped me down with such courtly manners that I almost laughed in spite of my nervousness.

"Jake," I said, "I want to thank you for rescuing me. And I'm sorry — very sorry — that I deceived you as I did. Please forgive me."

To my surprise, he turned as red as a beet. "Don't you worry about that, Miss Judith. I've been talking to Jeff and he explained it all to me. You kind of bowled us all over last night, but I think you're one spunky little lady."

My spirits soared. "Thank you, Jake. You don't know what it means to have one friend left among you."

"*One* friend?" His eyes widened, then narrowed. "Miss Judith —" He broke off at the approach of a tall, smiling man.

"Jake! It's good to see you here. Jeff tells me you have something to show me."

My embarrassment returned full flood. Some*thing,* indeed! Jake reached out eagerly to pump the man's hand. "Yep, we rounded up more than our share of strays this trip. Miss Judith, may I present Mr. Charles Bradley, owner of the Double B Ranch. Charles, this here is Miss Judith Alder, late of St. Joseph, and on her way to live with her uncle over in Taos."

Mr. Bradley took my extended hand and immediately endeared himself to me by ignoring my strange garb.

"Miss Alder, I am pleased to make your acquaintance. I hope you will do us the honor of being our guest for some time." He turned at the sound of approaching footsteps and smiled. Two women were walking toward us. The younger woman, slight and fair-haired, leaned on the arm of the older one, whose sharp, disapproving glance took in the group and focused on me.

"Allow me to present my wife, Abby," said Mr. Bradley. "Abby, Miss Alder." His wife was as gracious as her husband, smiling and completely overlooking my unconventional arrival. She released her hold on the older woman's arm and took a step toward her husband, who smiled and put a supporting arm around her waist.

"I'm glad to meet you, Miss Alder." Her voice was soft, and her speech bore evidence of a Southern origin.

The older woman stood as stiff and

straight as if she had swallowed a poker. Her eyes had not left my face since she first saw me, and they glittered now with animosity.

The Bradleys seemed to recall her presence. "My apologies," Mr. Bradley said, smiling. "Miss Alder, this is Mrs. Styles."

Her sharp eyes looked me up and down. I tentatively offered a hand, which she ignored. "And your family, Miss Alder? Are they stopping here also?"

Somehow I felt instinctively that the Bradleys wouldn't blink at my strange situation, but I hated to explain in front of Mrs. Styles. "I am not traveling with my family. I was on my way west when the people I was with deserted me. These trail drivers were kind enough to bring me here until I can make arrangements to finish my journey."

"And how long have you been in their company . . . alone?"

I made an effort to speak evenly. "I have been with them for two nights and two days, and all of them have behaved as perfect gentlemen." I put as much dignity into this speech as I could, considering that I was hardly dressed as the perfect lady.

Mrs. Styles sniffed and looked me up and down. "I shall be on my way, Abby. I will return to see you and Charles at a later date." She gave me a final scathing look and walked to a buggy standing in front of the house.

The four of us — the Bradleys, Jake, and I — let out a collective sigh of relief and looked at one another guiltily.

"Please, Miss Alder — may I call you Judith?" said Mrs. Bradley. "And you're to call us Charles and Abby. Things aren't nearly as formal here as they are back east. Don't be too upset by Lucia Styles. It's just that she has exceptionally high standards, and so few of us manage to live up to them." Her pale cheek dimpled as she smiled mischievously.

"Won't you come in and sit with me? I believe I need to rest a bit." She certainly looked it. The hand resting on her husband's arm was trembling.

"I'm sorry, dear," he said in a stricken voice. "I'll take you in at once." And with that, he swept her up in his arms. He turned to me. "She only came out to greet the drovers. She isn't supposed to be up for long periods. Please do come in. You must be exhausted."

I took my first look at the ranch house as I followed them inside. It was huge, a long, low, rambling affair of stone. Off to the west, the sun sank toward the horizon in a glorious array of pink and gold, its last brilliant rays picking out the soft hues in the stone walls. Different styles of building seemed to be represented, as though several additions had been made to the original structure, but all in all the effect was one of strength and permanence.

The house stood on a level area at the top of a low hill, commanding the view for miles in all directions. In the distance, cattle dotted the slopes.

Inside, the house was furnished elegantly and with taste, making one feel at home immediately without any hint of pretentiousness. Charles laid Abby gently on a couch, arranging cushions at her back to let her rest comfortably.

I sank gratefully into a deep chair he pointed out to me. It was my first taste of comfort in many days, and I felt as if I could sit there forever.

A plump woman in a gingham dress brought in a tea service, and Charles poured out steaming cups for the three of us.

"Now, Judith," he said, "you say your party deserted you along the trail?"

I retold my story for what seemed the thousandth time while we sat sipping our tea. I went back to Aunt Phoebe's choice of the Parkers to deliver me to Taos and omitted nothing along the way, including my decision to wear Lanny's clothes. Abby's dimple deepened at that, but she said nothing.

"And so they brought me here, and it appears they have decided I'm to stay with you until I can contact Uncle Matthew to make further arrangements. But I don't want to impose."

Abby laughed softly. "Judith, if you only knew how I welcome your company! Of course you must stay with us. Charles, please show her to a room and have Vera bring her plenty of hot water. I still have some dresses that haven't been taken in. She can try them on." She added to me, "I think you're much the same size I was before I lost weight."

I followed Charles down a long corridor to my room. He stopped at an open doorway. "Please make yourself at home, Judith. I'll see Vera about the water and Abby's dresses."

The room carried the same stamp of elegant simplicity that I had noted before, nothing lavish, but everything comfortable and lovely. The bed drew my attention first, and I settled myself gingerly on a corner. The mattress felt wonderfully soft and tempting, especially after so many days of bedrolls on the ground. I didn't dare lie upon it now, or I was sure I wouldn't move until morning.

A small overstuffed chair sat in one corner next to the stone fireplace, and a wardrobe and dresser stood on the other side of the room. The bed, chair, and floor had been covered with bright rugs, which I guessed were Indian in design and added a warm glow of color to the room.

There was a knock on the door, and the plump woman came into the room, carrying an armful of clothing. She was followed by two young boys, one bearing a bathtub and the other buckets of steaming water. The boys set down their cargo and left, but the woman lingered behind.

"Charles said to bring you dresses, but I figured you'd need more'n that, so I brought along some necessaries, too." She grinned and produced an array of undergarments from beneath the pile of dresses.

"That's very thoughtful." I smiled back at her. It was easy to relax in the face of her good humor.

She hefted the buckets as though they weighed nothing and poured them into the bath. "Soap's over there." She nodded toward the far wall, where a small table held a basin and pitcher.

"After you get all clean, I'll come if you want me to and help you try on the dresses. If they need some taking up or letting out, I can do that, too. But they should be pretty close. Abby used to be just about your size."

"Is she . . ." I trailed off, not knowing exactly how to ask about my frail hostess.

Vera understood. "No one's sure what's ailing her. She just started wasting away about six months ago. Nobody knows why, but Charles is worried sick about her."

"But surely a doctor could help."

"Honey, we don't have a doctor handy. There've been a couple passing through, though, and neither one of them could find a thing wrong." Her eyes misted over. It was plain to see she was as worried about Abby as anyone.

"But what you need right now," she said briskly, "is a long soak, some supper, and bed. I'll quit talking and let you get on with it."

Left to myself, I peeled off Lanny's shirt and overalls and the rest of the clothes I had worn, now filthy. Bless Vera for having thought of the "necessaries"!

The hot water felt heavenly. I soaked and

scrubbed and rinsed, then scrubbed some more. I lathered up my hair and washed it until it squeaked and my scalp tingled. When the water began to cool, I got out and wrapped myself in one of the huge, fluffy towels Vera had brought. I used another to get as much water as I could out of my hair.

I sorted through the clothes on the bed. They were all well made, with the attention to detail that transforms an ordinary garment into one of distinction.

I had just finished putting on clean undergarments when Vera tapped on the door and came in.

"My land, there was a pretty girl under all that grime," she said with a chuckle.

Together we held up the dresses, and Vera helped me into one that took my fancy. It was a pale blue, simply made, which brought out the blue in my eyes that my father had always called cornflower. Vera provided a supply of hairpins, and we dressed my still-damp hair into a simple style low on my neck.

"I need to see about supper," said Vera. "You come back to the parlor with me so you don't get lost your first night here."

Back in the parlor, I realized that despite the hearty helpings of beans, biscuits, and more beans I had eaten the last two days, I was famished for a home-cooked meal served at a table.

No one else was in the room, so I wandered around, admiring several of the different objects. My skirts rustled and swayed as I moved, a welcome feeling after having been encased in boy's clothes.

I sighed. Being clean again, wearing a dress, and once more looking like myself would have been enough, even without the Bradleys' kind hospitality. Their warm welcome, this lovely home, and the tempting smells drifting from the kitchen made the Parkers' perfidy and my masquerade fade away like a bad dream.

And I would not have to face the shunning of the cowboys any longer. I had known them only a short time, but I still did not like the thought of losing their respect.

I turned to see Charles Bradley standing in the open doorway, a pleased smile on his face. "You look refreshed, Judith. And that dress suits you admirably. Supper is ready now, but if you don't mind waiting a few moments more, my brother will join us."

I smiled back at him. "Thank you. I'm sure I can last that long. Is Abby feeling better?"

A shadow crossed his face. "She is having her supper on a tray in her room. I shouldn't have let her stay up and get so tired. But she was so excited about the rest of the cattle arriving safely that I thought it might do her good." He smiled again. "For all of her frailty now, Abby loved being involved in the ranch and the life that goes with it."

"I can see how she would. You have a beautiful home and a perfect setting for it. I want to thank you for your hospitality, especially to an unexpected guest. I do hope I won't need to impose on you for more than a short time."

"Please feel free to stay as long as you like. Both Abby and I are delighted to have you. So now, you see, you're an invited guest and don't need to consider your stay an imposition."

"I'll try not to. But is there some way of sending a message to my uncle? He'll be expecting me soon, and I need to let him know where I am and ask him to arrange some kind of transportation for me."

"Of course. I know you must be concerned for him and anxious to finish your journey. If you'll write out your message tonight, I'll send it with one of my men to the stage station tomorrow morning. And now," he said, turning, "I believe I hear my brother coming."

Footsteps sounded in the corridor, and a tall man stepped into the room. I gasped and felt the warm blood rush to my cheeks.

"I believe you're already acquainted with my brother, Jefferson," Charles said.

Chapter 7

His brother! Our gazes met and held while I struggled to keep from gaping and to make some sense of this new development.

Charles looked confused. "I'm sorry. I thought you two had met. Miss Alder, my brother, Jefferson Bradley."

"No, you're right, Charles. We have met," said his brother, the corners of his mouth twitching. "But it appears neither one of us made our identity quite clear."

Charles's brow furrowed again and Jeff laughed. "Don't worry, I'll explain later. Right now, I'm sure Miss Alder must be as hungry as I am. Let's go in to dinner."

The aroma from the kitchen had awakened a delicious anticipation of the supper to come. But after meeting Mr. Je— Bradley, I corrected myself — I could not have told what we ate.

The brothers were clearly delighted to be together again but made every effort to include me in their conversation. I appreciated their attempt to smooth over the awkwardness we all felt and soon became caught up in their discussion of the ranch.

"Something puzzles me," I ventured. "I always thought cattle were driven *from* the ranch *to* the market. But you brought thousands of them here."

Charles answered my question. "You're right, Judith. This is a little out of the ordinary. You have to understand that we grew up ranching in Texas and built up quite a herd. But times aren't easy in Texas these days. Abby and I moved up here a little over a year ago and brought half our herd with us. Jeff kept the rest in Texas in case the experiment failed.

"But this New Mexico Territory is open and fresh and ready for new blood. The cattle thrive here. And best of all, the railroad will extend this far west in just a few years, and we'll be able to drive cattle to a railhead in a matter of days, instead of taking them all the way up the trail to Abilene."

"So now you've brought all your livestock up here?"

"That's what we've done. We're sure now that the land will support the cattle, and Jeff and the hands we had left drove the rest of them here. Your arrival along with them was a pleasant surprise, eh, Jeff?"

"She was certainly a surprise," Jeff replied drily.

I chose not to rise to the bait.

After dinner, Charles excused himself to check on the new stock. Jeff walked with me as far as the parlor.

"It's a little different, seeing you like this," he said, smiling.

I ducked my head in confusion. "I'm really sorry about the mix-up. I never meant to —"

"I didn't mean that as a criticism," he said. "It's a nice difference."

"Thank you."

"You said you overheard me talking to Cookie last night?"

I nodded. "I couldn't help it. I don't eavesdrop as a rule."

"I just want you to know that . . . all the things Cookie said about you . . . I still think they're true." He cleared his throat. "Good night." And then he was gone.

I floated down the corridor to my room. Trying to think sensibly, I told myself that a total stranger had only said I had spunk, that I was game. It should hardly have produced such a heady sensation. I climbed into bed feeling ridiculously happy.

Next morning, after eating the breakfast Vera brought to my room on a tray, I dressed in another of Abby's dresses, a flowered print this time, and sat down to compose a note to Uncle Matthew, explaining my plight. With that done, I managed to find my way to the front of the house.

Charles was at one end of the broad porch, talking to his brother, while Abby lay in a hammock at the other. I felt my cheeks grow warm at the sight of Jeff and hurried to a chair next to Abby, hoping the others had not noticed.

She smiled. "That dress looks charming on you. I'm so glad you are able to wear it."

"It was good of you to lend your dresses to me. I'll return them once I've reached my uncle and can make more."

"No, don't worry about that. I'd like for you to have them. I have plenty for myself now, and I'm not likely to need that size again." A swift shadow crossed her face, to be replaced by her gentle smile.

"Don't look so distressed, Judith. Vera said she told you about my illness. I would like to grow well again, of course, but I know the Lord as my Savior, and I'm sure of a home in heaven if I don't recover."

Her gaze rested on her husband lovingly. "It's Charles that concerns me most. Charles and the children."

"Children?" I don't know why that should have surprised me, but I had seen no evidence of them, and it only seemed to compound the tragedy.

"We have two," she said, laughing, "although they get into so much mischief that sometimes it seems like more.

"Charles is so busy running the ranch, he can't spend as much time with them as he'd like, and Vera has all she can handle managing the house. Since I've been ill, I'm afraid they've run rather wild." The shadow crept into her eyes again. "It's for them that I mind the most."

I tried to think of something to say. Surely there were words of comfort, but they eluded me. Her faith touched me deeply, and I was grateful that she knew the Lord.

Would I be able to face death as calmly as she, even though it meant leaving a beloved family? I wondered.

She seemed to sense my distress, for she smiled again and tactfully changed the subject. "Tell me," she said, her eyes twinkling, "how did the men react when they found out you were a young lady instead of a boy?"

I groaned. "It certainly wasn't what I expected. I was prepared for all kinds of recriminations, but when it came down to it, I don't believe one of them actually said a word. Except Jeff, of course. Even Jake kept away from me after that until we arrived here.

"They must have been even more embarrassed than I was, but I still felt bad that they were all so angry they wouldn't even speak to me."

"Angry?" Abby raised an eyebrow. "Judith, is this your first trip west?" I nodded. "Well, brace yourself, my dear. I think you're in for a surprise."

Before I could ask what she meant, Charles and Jeff came up behind us. Charles smoothed his wife's hair tenderly. "Did you write your message to your uncle?" he asked me. I took the note from my pocket and handed it to him. "One of the men is leaving for town soon. I'll send it along with him," he promised.

Abby looked up at Jeff and smiled. "Welcome home," she said. "I didn't get a chance to greet you last night. I hope you were comfortable."

Jeff grinned back at her. "After all those nights on the trail, anything would have been an improvement. But my bed felt wonderful, Abby. The place already feels like home."

"Did Charles tell you the news?"

"Nothing but news since I got here. Was there any particular thing you had in mind?"

Abby made a face at him, and I gathered that the lighthearted banter between these three was of long standing. I wondered if this was too tiring for Abby, but her color seemed improved and her manner more relaxed.

"Why *the* news, of course. Just in time for your arrival, we have acquired a minister at Three Forks."

Jeff whistled and a grin broke out on his face. I felt my heart quicken and told myself it was due to the news and his infectious grin. I would surely be here at least throughout the weekend. How wonderful it would be to attend a worship service again before traveling on!

"How did you manage that?" Jeff asked.

"Really, he just fell into our laps," answered Charles. "He had to give up his church in the east because of ill health and traveled out here under his doctor's orders. If the climate suits him, he may stay permanently."

"Wouldn't that be fine!" Jeff's eyes

glowed with a happiness that — I checked myself. I was becoming all too interested in the moods of a stranger, even one who had rescued me. I would be gone in a few days to a new life filled with new people. The thought should not have left me feeling so bleak.

I forced my attention back to the conversation. ". . . only had time to shake his hand and say hello," Charles was saying. "But this western air should make a new man out of him, if he'll stay long enough to give it a chance."

He broke off and frowned, sniffing. There *was* a peculiar smell, sweet and cloying, even though we were outside. We were all looking for its source when Shorty and Neil stepped around the corner of the house, bringing an even stronger cloud of the scent with them. They stopped before us and shuffled their feet.

"What on earth!" sputtered Charles. "Did you two tangle with a skunk this morning? Back away so the rest of us can breathe, won't you?"

Shorty looked hurt. "Aw, Boss, you ain't making fun of my cologne, are you?"

"Cologne?" Charles stepped down off the porch and circled the pair slowly. "Hair combed," he said in awe. "Clean shaven, and, I declare, I believe those shirts have been washed sometime within the last six months. What's gotten into you boys?" Behind me, I heard Abby giggle.

"Why, Boss," said Shorty, with an attempt at wounded dignity, "we just came in off the trail and wanted to make ourselves presentable. Right, Neil?"

Neil, his gaze fastened on the toe of his boot, mumbled assent.

"And being naturally kindhearted, we thought we'd come and see how Miss Judith was doing this morning. We wanted to see if there was anything we could do for her. Right, Neil?"

Neil gulped and nodded.

"I see," Charles said kindly. "I appreciate that, boys, and I'm sure Miss Alder does, too. As a matter of fact," he continued, "there is something you could do, but it's a job for just one of you."

Shorty stepped forward. "I'm your man," he announced.

"Good for you," Charles said. "Take this message to the stage station at Three Forks. It's on the trail, about fifteen miles southwest of here. You can't miss it."

Shorty stared, crestfallen, as Charles handed him the note and gave him a hearty clap on the shoulder. He looked mournfully at the paper, then shook his head and started toward the corral.

Charles turned his attention to Neil. "Well, what's keeping you from your chores?"

Neil turned brick red and stared intently at his boot. "Begging your pardon, Boss, but I twisted my ankle something awful this morning, and I thought maybe I ought to sit down and give it a chance to heal." He looked up at Charles hopefully. "Like maybe on the porch?"

Charles rolled his eyes skyward. Neil heaved a sigh and walked away with a pronounced limp I was sure had not been evident earlier. Jeff and Charles watched him go, then walked off toward the corral, chuckling.

I sat wide-eyed through this performance, unable to utter a word, but now I turned to Abby. "Was that really for my benefit?"

She nodded, still trying to control her laughter. Evidently, her illness had not dampened her sense of humor. "Oh, Judith!" she burst out, "I knew your coming here would do me good, but what havoc you've wrought on these poor cowboys!"

I sighed. If nothing else, my presence here seemed to be highly entertaining to everyone else. No, I shouldn't feel sorry for myself. If I could do anything at all to lighten Abby's spirits, I would.

We talked on in the warm sunshine. A light breeze stirred from time to time. Abby told me of her girlhood in Virginia as the youngest daughter of a wealthy plantation owner and of her family's dismay when she married and left with Charles, who had been visiting relatives nearby.

"They told me I would regret marrying 'beneath me,'" she said. "But I've never regretted one instant with Charles. Judith, I hope that when the time is right, you will find someone who will make you as happy as I have been." Her eyes sparkled with mischief. "You realize, of course, that you have only to say the word to have the pick of any of the cowboys on the ranch."

I pretended to consider the matter. "Shorty, perhaps? No, I don't think I'd care to go through life wondering if a skunk was going to creep up on me in my sleep." We both laughed.

When Abby felt she could walk a bit, she showed me around the house. The arrangement was much less complicated than I had thought. The house was made up of four wings forming a hollow square, in the center of which was a spacious courtyard.

Nearly all the rooms in the house opened onto the courtyard, except for a few, including mine, which were located in a sort of annex that projected beyond one corner of the square. The annex itself was connected to the courtyard by means of a covered walkway that separated the north and west wings.

A tall cottonwood tree grew in the center of the courtyard, with a bench encircling it. Bright flowers bloomed near a well, and two sets of hitching rails flanked a large gate set in the east wall.

"How lovely," I breathed. "It's like having your own little world."

"It is peaceful here," Abby agreed. "It started out as a trading post, and they had to build it almost like a fortress for protection. The fur trade started to die out, so it was sold several years ago to an Englishman. He had a substantial amount of money but, as a younger son, no hope of inheriting property in England. So he bought this place and transformed it from a trading post into a showplace.

"He added onto the original building. I rather imagine he planned to build more on bit by bit and create his own 'ancestral home.' By the time he finished the annex, he'd grown lonely and bored and went back to England, where he could spend his money in a more populous area."

"And then you moved here?"

She nodded. "When we first saw it, it seemed like home. Charles and Jeff were determined to leave Texas so we could have a better life, and it seemed this place was here just waiting for us."

We were interrupted by Vera's call to lunch. Today, I joined Abby for the meal, which she ate in her room. She seemed to have enjoyed the conversation and walk, but she tired so quickly, she explained, that it was easier for all concerned if she could eat and go immediately to bed for a midday rest.

The next few days fell into a pattern. I would spend the morning visiting with Abby, then eat lunch with her and help her to bed. I usually took a brief rest at that time myself, then the rest of the afternoon was mine to use as I wished, exploring the immediate area or relaxing on the bench in the courtyard with a good book.

The fellowship with Abby was sweet, and I was grateful the Lord had given me this oasis of calm in the midst of the upheaval in my life. I wished, though, that Uncle

Matthew would hasten his reply. Despite the Bradleys' glad acceptance of my company, I had no wish to be a burden.

It was during my third afternoon on my own that I became acquainted with the Bradley children. I ventured out the gate and walked for some distance, reveling in the view and the pure air. Surely, I felt, in such vast surroundings, a person ought to expand in character to match it.

I made my way back to the house and was passing through the wide gate when something hard was pressed into my back.

My knees went weak. Abby's words came back to me: fortress, protection. This was still wild country. How could I have forgotten?

A voice behind me piped, "Hands up, and don't try anything."

Piped? Either I had been accosted by a soprano ruffian or . . . I took a chance and turned my head. I had to drop my gaze to come in contact with those of my assailant, who was holding a stick rifle in the small of my back and trying to maintain a stern expression.

Another small figure moved from behind the gate and stood beside the first. Both wore rough clothing, a miniature replica of the cowboys' garb. Both wore hats several sizes too large pulled down over their eyes and held wooden rifles. And both glowered at me.

The smaller one spoke first. "See, Lizzie, you spoiled it! If you hadn't gone and talked, it would've been fine. She turned just as white as a sheet."

I knelt down in front of them and raised their hat brims so I could look into their faces. "What on earth were you two doing?"

Again, it was the smaller one who broke the silence. "We were bein' outlaws. And if Lizzie here hadn't of opened her mouth, I bet we could have gotten all your money. You were really scared, weren't you?"

"As a matter of fact," I admitted, "I was. How did two youngsters like you learn to be outlaws?"

"Aw, we hang around the bunkhouse a lot," said my young informant. "They tell real good stories, and they don't mind us bein' there, as long as we keep quiet. They even let Lizzie stay around, and she's a girl." He lowered his voice conspiratorially. "Even if she don't dress like one."

At this, Lizzie found her voice. "I don't have to dress any different if I don't want to!" she shouted. "Shorty said I look fine just like I am. He said it didn't matter if I didn't want to wear girl clothes. He said . . . he said there was a lot of that going around," she ended on a defiant note.

It was time to change the subject. "All right. I know you're Lizzie. My name is Judith." I looked over at the other aspiring outlaw. "Now, what's your name?"

"That's Willie," Lizzie answered. "He's my little brother. Our last name is Bradley. What's yours?"

"Alder," I said, trying to come to terms with the fact that these little hoodlums belonged to Charles and Abby.

I wondered if Abby was aware of just how wild they had become. I had been under the impression that they were cared for during the day in a part of the house where their noise wouldn't disturb her rest. Apparently they ran loose, unattended. Hanging around the bunkhouse, indeed! I could imagine the kind of stories they were likely to overhear.

This, I realized, *could be a way to repay Charles and Abby in part for their kindness in letting me stay.* If I could do nothing else, I could at least look after the well-being of their children while I was here.

"Why don't you both come with me," I said, rising. "We'll see about cleaning your hands and faces, then we'll try to find something for you to eat while you tell me about those outlaws you seem to like so well."

To my surprise, they each took one of my hands and walked along docilely to my room, where I poured water into the basin and scrubbed their hands and faces until they fairly shone.

"Underneath all that dust, you were hiding some very good-looking children," I said, surveying my work with satisfaction. Willie was a miniature of his father, with a naturally cheerful expression not even his assumed scowl could hide. Lizzie had her mother's fair hair, but along with that went the determined Bradley chin I had noticed on her uncle.

They both stood and stared at me. I thought of how their lives must have changed over the past few months, with their mother suddenly unable to care for them and their father busy building up a new ranch. Everyone was so occupied with their own duties that the children were, for the most part, forgotten.

The poor things were trying to adjust to the upheaval without any consistent guidance. They had been passive enough about doing as I had bidden, but it was little wonder they were reluctant to open up to a stranger.

"How about something to eat?" I asked.

Vera had been in the habit of bringing a late-night snack of cookies and milk to my room, and I had some leftover cookies wrapped in a handkerchief in a dresser drawer. When they saw what I was offering, their faces lit up, and in no time the three of us were munching away at our impromptu tea party.

My heart went out to them. How long had it been since they had a bit of fun, I wondered. I discounted story hour in the bunkhouse. From my acquaintance with the cowboys, I felt certain it was not the sort of entertainment the children needed.

Having finished her cookies, Lizzie eyed me steadily. "That's my mama's dress," she announced. I nodded, wondering if she felt I had no right to be wearing it and whether I should explain. "It still smells a little like my mama," she said and, to my surprise, snuggled up next to me. I put my arm around her and blinked to keep back the tears.

"Wouldn't you like to go with me to your room, Lizzie, and pick out a dress for you to wear?" I was totally unprepared for her reaction.

"No!" she shouted. "I won't! If I wear a dress, everyone says I'm just like my mama. And I don't want to get sick like she is. I don't!" With that, she burst into sobs and buried her face in my lap. I stroked her fair hair and let her cry. She had to have some way to turn loose of the pain she had been carrying.

Willie looked on with a stoic expression until I tentatively held out a hand to him. Then he, too, snuggled into the circle of my arm, and the three of us huddled together in a tight little knot while Lizzie's sobs racked her small body and even Willie sniffled occasionally.

Poor little things! I held them even closer to me. Lizzie couldn't be more than nine years old, and Willie looked to be six or seven. I tried to picture the family as they must have been, with Abby caring for her children and Charles romping with them, before this wasting illness took its toll. Abby was right; she was not the only one to suffer.

I promised myself to bring up the subject gently with her at the first opportunity. She had told me the children ate their meals in the kitchen and that she seldom saw them until they were brought to her room at night, freshly scrubbed and ready for bed. I felt sure she believed they were being properly tended to, for I could not believe for a moment she would rest easy if she had any idea how much time they spent on their own.

The shadows were growing long by the time the emotional storm had subsided. I washed the children's hands and faces again and sent them along to the kitchen for their supper. I was touched by their reluctance to leave me and promised them we would spend more time together during my stay.

The next day was Saturday, and Abby took a turn for the worse. Charles turned full responsibility for the ranch over to Jeff and spent the day hovering over her. Vera, solemn-faced, rushed to and from her room with supplies and tonics I gathered had been left by the doctors she had mentioned.

I felt utterly useless. I tried to find the children but was informed they had been taken for a ride in order to spare them the tension of the day. So I found myself empty-handed and restless.

I decided to take a walk. Maybe the exercise would work off some of my own tension. How long had I been here? Was it only four days? And yet these people had become so dear to me that I hated the thought of being separated from them.

I sank down under a spreading cedar tree and prayed, first for Abby's recovery, then for my own situation. Would there ever again be a place where I truly belonged and had a right to stay?

The smells of summer were all around me, the scent of the scrub brush and the dusty ground where I sat. The land rolled away from me, the grasses waving in the gentle wind. Off in the distance, I could see groups of cattle, and here and there a rider appeared against the skyline. It was a calm, pastoral scene, belying the worry in the house and the tumult within me.

I stayed under my cedar until most of the afternoon had passed, alternately praying and wondering what the future held in store. When the sun was well down in the sky, I stood, dusted myself off, and turned back toward the house.

Jeff's figure loomed in the open gateway as I approached, and I hurried toward him, fear mounting within me. "Abby," I faltered. "Is she . . . ?"

"She's resting," he said, and I sighed with relief. His mouth curved in one of his slow smiles. "I didn't mean to frighten you. I wondered where you were, and nobody had seen you for some time, so I thought I'd make sure you were all right."

"I wanted to stay out of the way, and I was worried about Abby, so I went for a walk," I said, lowering my gaze to hide my pleasure at his concern.

"It's been rough on you, hasn't it? Have you had any word from your uncle?"

I shook my head and raised my eyes to search his. "Shouldn't I have heard something by now? It seems to me a stagecoach would have had time to get there and back."

"That would be cutting it pretty close. And if there were any problems at all, it could delay your message, or his, or both."

"What kind of problems?"

"This is still new country. A lot of things can happen. But I wouldn't be too concerned just yet. Give it a few more days."

He walked with me to the door of my room. "I'll have supper sent to you. What with all the worry over Abby, our routine is a bit off today."

"Of course. Isn't there something I can do? Maybe sit with her tonight?"

He shook his head. "Charles will insist on doing that himself. They're devoted to each other, as I'm sure you've noticed. I just hope this doesn't last too long. He's about done in, what with trying to handle the ranch alone and worrying about her on top of it. I wish you had known her before she got sick."

He seemed lost in thought for a moment, then pulled himself together. "Well, I'll see you tomorrow," he said. He turned as if to leave, then hesitated. "Judith? I know Charles and Abby won't be up to going into town for church in the morning. But if you'd like to go, I'd be happy to drive you."

"All right," I said. "I'd love to go." I entered my room before he could see the foolish grin that spread across my face. It wasn't until I was almost asleep that I realized he had called me by my Christian name for the first time.

Chapter 8

By the next morning, it was clear that Abby was going to rally, and I readied myself for my first church service in weeks. Could it be possible that only a week before I had been rolling along in a wagon with the Parkers for company?

I hummed a happy little tune as I tried to decide which dress to wear. Truly, there was a great deal to be thankful for on this Lord's Day.

I chose a sprigged muslin with ruffles at the wrists and throat. Vera had thoughtfully provided a number of hairpins, so I was able to dress my hair more elaborately than usual.

I looked in the mirror for a final appraisal and saw a sparkle in my eyes and a pink flush on my cheeks, due, I assured myself, to the excitement of going to a church service. How wonderful it would be to worship in company with other believers and hear the Bible taught by this learned man from the East!

Muffins and coffee were waiting in the kitchen. Everyone was too tired from the strain of the day before to care much about a formal meal.

A glance out the window showed a team and wagon approaching the house, so I gathered up my Bible and a light shawl and hurried outdoors. Jeff sprang down to help me up to the wagon seat and handed me my shawl.

"We'll be all set as soon as our other passengers are ready," he said, smiling up at me. Good heavens! Up to then I had completely forgotten the need for a chaperon. I smiled to cover my confusion and said a silent prayer of thanks that he was gentleman enough to have thought of it as a matter of course. After my experiences on the trail, I knew I would be perfectly safe with him or any of the cowboys, but we were heading for civilization of sorts, where tongues would wag if given half a chance.

I turned at the sound of footsteps and drew a quick breath in astonished delight. Lizzie and Willie stood beside the wagon, scrubbed and dressed in their Sunday best.

Willie looked gentlemanly, if uncomfortable, with his stiff collar and slicked-down hair. And Lizzie was the very picture of an angel with her hair neatly combed and in, wonder of wonders, a dainty ruffled dress. Jeff lifted them into the back of the wagon, where they scooted up behind the seat and looked at me shyly.

"One more and we'll be off," said Jeff. I looked at him in surprise. Neither Abby nor Charles would be in any condition to stir today. Perhaps Vera was coming. A broad smile broke out on Jeff's face, and I followed his gaze to see Jake emerge from the bunkhouse and walk our way.

His hair was plastered as close to his head as Willie's, and he wore what must have been his best pair of work clothes. I hoped he hadn't felt it necessary to borrow Shorty's cologne.

His expression, his walk, his every move showed resignation rather than pleasure at the prospect of going to church. I couldn't quite suppress a smile at his hangdog look.

"Hurry up, cowpuncher," called Jeff. "We're ready to roll!"

"So help me, Jeff, I don't see why you needed someone to come along to play nursemaid," Jake muttered, his gaze gloomily fastened on the ground. "Seems to me you ought to be able to handle a couple of half-pints by yourself."

"Why, Jake," Jeff said, all innocence, "I asked for one of you boys to volunteer to come along this morning. Do you mean you aren't here by choice? I really do need you. You see, I have three on my hands instead of two."

"Three?" Jake looked up at his employer for the first time, then glanced around. His gaze lit on me and his jaw dropped ludicrously. "Excuse me, ma'am," he sputtered. "I surely didn't know any young lady was going or I wouldn't have talked so."

"Good morning, Jake," I said demurely. "I've missed your company."

He peered up at me, squinting, then his eyes grew round in surprise. "Will ya look at that!" he exclaimed. "If it ain't Miss Judith!"

If I needed any gratification for my feminine vanity, I couldn't have asked for more than Jake's reaction. He climbed silently into the back of the wagon and sat, shaking his head from time to time.

It wasn't until we had driven a mile or so that he began to chuckle softly. The chuckles increased until he was leaning against the side of the wagon, his head thrown back and tears streaming down his cheeks.

"All right," said Jeff. "Better tell us what

it is before you hurt something."

Jake pulled a bandanna from his back pocket and mopped at his face. "It's . . . it's seein' Miss Judith up there lookin' like that," he said, gasping for breath. "Won't Shorty be sore when he finds out who I'm goin' to church with?"

"I don't understand," I said. "Why should Shorty be angry?"

"He's the one that slipped me the short straw when we were deciding who was going to 'volunteer'!" And he went off again into gales of laughter.

Jeff looked at me as if wondering how I would react to learning I was the loser's lot. When our eyes met, we both laughed heartily. The children, too, joined in the general merriment, and the slight tension that had been present dissolved.

The drive into town took about three hours in the wagon, and we whiled away a good bit of the time singing hymns. Jeff had a pleasant baritone and started us off on song after song in seemingly endless procession.

I was pleased to find I knew most of the hymns he sang and could join in with him. What Jake's voice lacked in quality, he made up for in enthusiasm on the songs he knew and on some he didn't. The children,

I noted with approval, knew a good many of the hymns. I made a mental note to teach them one or two more before I left.

The settlement was small, not much more than a store, a warehouse, two saloons, and a dozen houses along a wide, dusty street.

Jeff drew the team to a halt in front of the store and checked his watch. "Thirty minutes to spare," he announced with satisfaction. "That gives us a chance to look the place over."

Jake stared wistfully at the nearest saloon. "I don't suppose . . . ," he began.

"Not today," Jeff answered. "Today you are coming to church. Take Lizzie and Willie in and find us all a place to sit, will you?"

He grinned as he lifted me down from the seat. "This is hardly the way Jake planned to spend his Sunday. He's a good man — one of the best — but he relies too much on his own merit. Hearing a real man of God may be just what he needs to realize that no one can be 'good enough' on his own.

"Tell me," he went on, tucking my hand under his arm, "what kind of miracle have you worked on Lizzie and Willie? They've always had a mischievous streak, but as soon as they heard you were coming to church with me, they were wild to come along. They look positively angelic this morning. Vera tells me it's the first time Lizzie's worn a dress in months."

When I related my meeting with the children, his face sobered as he realized the depth of their feelings about their mother's illness. "Poor kids! I guess we've all been so busy that they've been 'out of sight, out of mind.' " He gave my hand a gentle squeeze. "It looks like your coming has been good for all of us."

I floated into the store where the service was to be held and had to make an effort to respond sensibly to the people I met. I shook hands with people whose names I barely heard and could not remember, until a familiar face loomed before me, and I recognized Mrs. Styles.

"Mr. Bradley," she said archly, "I am pleased to see you here this morning. Is Abby better? I drove out yesterday to visit her but was turned away most abruptly by one of your hands."

Jeff nodded politely and said, "She seems to be better today, thank you." He turned to walk on to our seats, but she stopped him.

"Come now, aren't you going to introduce me to your charming companion? We don't see many fresh young faces around here, you know."

"But I thought you had already met her. This is Miss Judith Alder, Mrs. Styles. She's a guest at the ranch."

The smile froze on her face and she peered at me more closely.

"Oh," she said. "Oh!" She withdrew the hand she had extended, turned stiffly, and marched to a seat on the front row of chairs.

The encounter brought my feet back to earth with an effective thud. We spotted Jake. He had found seats for all of us on the last row, which suited me fine. I sat between the children, leaving the two men to flank us.

Jake leaned across Lizzie and whispered hopefully, "The place is fillin' up, don't you think? Maybe I ought to slip on out and give other folks a chance to sit down."

Jeff responded with a look that made him sit back in his chair, shoulders slumped. It would have been funny if I hadn't felt so mortified. Mrs. Styles had obviously formed a most unflattering opinion of me. I would have to be careful to behave in an exemplary manner around her.

A hush fell as a middle-aged man stood and led the congregation in singing hymns. I tried to recapture the joy of worship I had anticipated, but the mood wouldn't come.

You're being ridiculous, I scolded myself. *Letting yourself get caught up in romantic notions when you're only going to be here a short while! If you're not careful, Judith Alder, you'll appear to be just what Lucia Styles thinks you are.*

That was enough to settle my thoughts in preparation for the sermon. Wasn't this why we had come — to hear a man of God bring a message from the Word?

I deliberately focused my attention on the man who now stood at the front of the worshippers. He was younger than I expected, probably around Charles Bradley's age, and the black frock coat he wore accented the pallor of his skin. He had come west, I remembered, for his health.

"Welcome, my friends," he intoned. "As many of you good people know, I am the Reverend Thomas Carver from Philadelphia, Pennsylvania. I have come to this savage land seeking a climate conducive to recovery and have agreed to preach in your quaint settlement this Sunday. If we find each other satisfactory, I will consider lengthening my stay to help you profit from the knowledge I have acquired."

I felt a stab of disappointment, though I could not pinpoint the cause. His preaching style was different from what I was accustomed to, that was all.

He was quite slender, as might be expected of one who had recently been ill. His face was long and narrow, the features almost delicate. His hair was a very light blond, and his eyebrows and lashes must have been as well, for from my seat I could not distinguish them. He was, I judged, in his early thirties — still a young man but old enough to have had experience in the pulpit.

I heard the rustle of pages and realized that he had announced the Scripture text for his sermon, and I had not been paying attention. I peered over Willie's head at Jeff's Bible, trying to see what page he had turned to. Isaiah 61. I hastily turned there myself.

" 'The Spirit of the Lord God is upon me; because the Lord hath anointed me to preach good tidings unto the meek; he hath sent me to bind up the broken-hearted, to proclaim liberty to the captives, and the opening of the prison to them that are bound; To proclaim the acceptable year of the Lord . . .' "

The words lingered in my mind as the Reverend Carver stood for a moment, surveying the congregation. He sighed as if disappointed in what he saw, then took a deep breath and began.

"Brethren," he said, "I see unhappy faces here among you. I see faces lined with bitterness and despair. Why? Why are you discouraged? Why do you feel you have failed in some way? Because, my friends, you have succumbed to the philosophy of many that there is no inherent goodness in man."

There was a stirring among those present, whether of interest or antagonism I could not tell. I was having a difficult enough time trying to concentrate on what he was saying rather than on the rise and fall of my emotions.

Really, I chided myself sternly, *whatever is troubling you can wait until after the service. An opportunity for spiritual feeding may not come often in these parts.*

"Certainly there are those who do not treat others as they should, those who are bad neighbors, those who fall into crime. But why are they this way? I tell you, it is not due to any evil within themselves but to the lack of love given them from parents, friends, society itself!

"Friends, no one ever bothered to look for the good that is in them, to bring it out and nurture it. And how can they love others if they do not love themselves first and foremost? Therein lies the key to the evils in this world. Many have failed to look for the good."

Even my wandering attention was held by this. The sermon went on interminably in the same vein, seeking to point out man's innate goodness.

I wondered if anyone else was bothered by the lack of concern with sin and man's unrighteousness. A quick glance to my left showed Jeff's mouth set in a thin line. I relaxed a little. So it wasn't only my own perception.

It was an effort to stay awake until the end of the service, too much effort for Lizzie and Willie, who slumped against me and slept.

After the final prayer, people rose and milled around, talking quietly. The Reverend Carver positioned himself at the door to greet the worshippers as they left. As I tried to wake the children, I couldn't help but notice that while the preacher's comments were enthusiastic, the responses he got were lukewarm at best.

By the time we were ready to leave, there were only a couple of men left in the store putting away the chairs. I took a drowsy Lizzie by the hand and started for the door, wishing there were another exit.

The Reverend Carver smiled at Lizzie, who glared at him. He then turned to me. "Ah, Miss Alder, is it not?" he asked with a wonderful display of white teeth. I managed a nod. "Mrs. Styles has told me a great deal about you."

I hope you told her to look for the good, I thought rebelliously.

He went on without bothering to lower his voice. "I believe you were stranded alone on the trail and arrived here under the, ah, protection of a group of trail drivers. Is that correct?"

I looked around frantically, not wanting my experience to be overheard and misinterpreted by the whole town. "As I told Mrs. Styles," I said in a low voice, "they were kindness itself and absolute gentlemen."

Behind me, Jake and Jeff had given up trying to rouse Willie, and Jake was carrying him out. "These are two of the men who helped me," I told the minister, turning gratefully to Jeff, who was by this time at my elbow. "This is Mr. Bradley. I believe you have met his brother."

"Of course, of course. Good morning, Mr. Bradley. I hope you enjoyed the service." I didn't hear Jeff's reply, as I had propelled Lizzie toward the wagon at the first opportunity and now stood leaning against it.

The morning had started out with such promise; now even the brightness of the noonday seemed to have dimmed. Mrs. Styles alone had been bad enough, but knowing that she had spread her version of my arrival made me want to crawl under the blanket on the wagon bed and remain there until we were out of town.

The pastor's inflection left no doubt in my mind as to the picture that had been painted of me. I thought of the people I met before the service. My head had been too much in the clouds at the time to take note of their reaction, but now I wondered. Had there been a hidden meaning behind the smiles and friendly words? Suddenly, I couldn't wait to get away.

I hoisted Lizzie to the wagon bed, gave her orders to sit quietly, and scrambled to the seat. If only the men would hurry! I imagined curtains being drawn back furtively to take a look at the questionable newcomer.

To my intense relief, Jake and Jeff came striding toward the wagon at that moment and arranged a comfortable place in the back for Willie, who was snoring gently.

Jeff had just settled onto the seat beside me when a man ran out of the store, waving at us.

"Miss Alder?" he said. "I'm Fred Kilmer. I run the general store. I have a letter here for you, but I didn't realize who you were until the Reverend Carver pointed you out."

My cheeks burned as I envisioned the scene, but I reached for the letter with hope rising in my heart. "Thank you," I said as we pulled away.

Joyfully, I tore at the envelope. I need not stay here to suffer further humiliation. Soon I would be heading west once more to begin my new life. I read:

Dear Judith,

Sorry to hear of your delay, but it may be for the best. There was a fire at the trading post. Burned the place clear to the ground. I don't have the money to rebuild and restock, so I'm off to find greener pastures. Glad to hear you have found a place where they're good to you. Stay put until I send for you. Don't know how soon it will be.

Your loving uncle,
Matthew

I stared at the paper. *Stay put?* Tears stung my eyes and blurred the landscape. How could I stay? I could not presume indefinitely on the Bradleys' hospitality. I had no money to pay for my board, either there or in town. And the thought of remaining, to be an object of community scorn, filled me with dread.

The only course that seemed open to me was one I dreaded as much as Mrs. Styles's wagging tongue. I could wire Aunt Phoebe, throw myself on her mercy, and beg for forgiveness and my passage back home.

I knew that would end any further hopes of going west to be with Uncle Matthew. My rebellion in doing so once would never be forgotten.

We were over halfway back to the ranch when Jeff spoke. "Have you had bad news?" he asked softly. I handed him the brief letter, which he scanned and handed back.

"I'm sorry," he said. "You've had a hard time of it lately." I nodded, too miserable to speak.

He turned his head toward the back of the wagon. I followed his gaze. Lizzie had curled up next to her brother, and Jake leaned against the wagon's side, head back and eyes closed.

"Do you want to talk about it?"

I struggled to force words past the obstruction in my throat. "I guess the only thing for me to do is go back to Missouri, to my aunt."

"And try again when your uncle has relocated?"

I shook my head and managed a small laugh. "No. I'm afraid this will be my first and last trip west. Once I go back, my aunt will see to it that I never leave St. Joseph again."

He stared straight ahead. "Will that really be so bad? It isn't civilized out here yet, at least not in the way you're used to."

"But I like what I've seen. There's a wildness here, a bigness that's almost frightening, but I want — wanted — to be a part of it."

"Then why go back?"

"It's the only thing I can do. I have no choice." A warm breeze rustled the grasses and played with loose strands of my hair, but the beauty of the day was lost on me as I stared at the rolling hills through tear-filmed eyes.

When we reached the ranch, Jeff took the children to see their mother, and I closeted myself in my room. I lay facedown on the bed, trying to adjust to the idea of returning to a way of life I thought I had left forever.

My brain was numb, unable to deal with the blow I had received. Could I go back again to being the poor relation, tolerated only because of a blood tie? My whole being rebelled at the thought, but what else was there?

The return of the prodigal. That's how Aunt Phoebe would see it. But there would be no joyous welcome, no fatted calf. It would be back to life as usual, dancing attendance on Aunt Phoebe and being the object of disdain among the ladies of her circle. They would have plenty to fuel their imaginations as they tried to figure out what I had really been up to during my absence.

The tidy streets of my aunt's neighborhood would be the same, yards neatly trimmed, picket fences faithfully whitewashed. It was the scene from my growing-up years, constant and unchanging since the day we came to live with Aunt Phoebe.

I closed my eyes wearily. In my mind's

eye, I could see the vast land outside the courtyard walls. It, too, had remained the same and for much longer than St. Joseph. But here, there was openness and freedom. The very landscape had a life of its own as it responded to the wind, rain, and sun. One could spend a lifetime here getting acquainted with the country, always discovering something new.

A figure appeared on my imaginary landscape, a figure who turned and looked at me with smiling blue eyes, called out a glad welcome, and waited with open arms for me to come. I shook myself back to reality and noticed how far the sun had moved across the sky. I must have been dozing.

I poured water into the basin and scrubbed at my face. I wanted to stay. But how? Resolve began to stiffen my drooping spine. I didn't know how, not yet. But for once in my life, I would fight for something I wanted.

Pacing the floor of my room, I began to make my plans. Surely I could find a job in town and a place to stay. Since I'd planned to help Uncle Matthew in his trading post, perhaps I could get a job helping Mr. Kilmer at the general store.

The more I mulled over the possibilities,

the more enthusiastic I became. Even the thought of Mrs. Styles and her venomous gossip could not dampen my mood. I knew I had done nothing wrong, and it was high time I started holding my head up.

For the first time in days, I felt sure of where my path led. I would stay. There would be no slinking off, no whimpering in defeat. This was where my heart lay. This was where I belonged.

I patted my hair into place and headed for the parlor, bursting with the need to tell someone about my plans. I nearly collided with Charles in the doorway. He looked tired, and I remembered how much sleep he must have lost caring for Abby. Perhaps because of that, he was quick in coming to the point.

"Jefferson tells me you're leaving us," he said without preamble.

"Yes, but —"

"Don't do it," he interrupted. He seemed to realize how brusque this sounded and made a visible effort to collect himself. "I mean, don't do it, *please*."

Still bubbling with my newly devised strategy, I didn't see at first what he was getting at. "Charles, I appreciate so much the hospitality you've shown me, but I can't abuse it. That's why I've decided —"

"Have you talked her out of it yet?" This time the interruption came from Jeff, who strode into the center of the room and stood clenching and unclenching his fists.

I stared from one brother to the other, trying to understand. Jeff seemed to sense my bewilderment.

"Charles, do you mean you haven't asked her yet?"

"You haven't given me much opportunity," Charles said mildly.

"Ask me what?" I nearly shouted. "Will someone please tell me what's going on?"

Jeff looked at me, then at his brother, turned on his heel, and was gone. I stared openmouthed at Charles.

He smiled and shook his head. "Please forgive us, Judith. We've both been under a great strain.

"I talked with my children a little while ago. Talked *and* listened for the first time in longer than I care to admit. I had no idea they'd been allowed to go unsupervised all this time.

"That leaves me in a dilemma. My time will be fully taken up for some time. Abby is in no condition to do anything but rest, and I have no people here whose work will allow them to take on the added responsibility for the children.

"Would you consider staying here to care for them, at least for a while? Until we send some cattle to market, all my transactions will be on credit, so I can't offer you more than room and board for the time being. But the children seem to like you a great deal, and you'd be doing us all a great favor — myself, Abby, and Jefferson."

"Jeff?"

"My brother is not ordinarily a highly strung person," he said with a smile. "But you saw him just now. And I've never seen him in as excitable a state as when he told me you were leaving and ordered me to find a way to keep you here."

I looked at him in surprise and he grinned back. "If Abby and I hadn't already decided to ask you to stay, I would have had to create a reason, just to pacify him.

"So what do you think, Judith? Could you put up with us all a little longer? Would you like some time to consider the matter?"

"No! I mean, yes. I mean . . . I'd be very happy to stay on. Thank you." I managed to contain myself until I got back to the privacy of my room, where I spun about with wild abandon. Jeff had demanded that Charles ask me to stay!

I could hardly contain my joy. He wanted me here!

Chapter 9

It was with a light heart that I was able to pen a letter to Aunt Phoebe, telling her of my safe arrival in New Mexico Territory, the unfortunate fire at Uncle Matthew's, and my temporary position with the Bradleys. I felt sorely tempted to give her my opinion of her carefully chosen chaperones, but I could so easily picture her deriving a perverse sense of satisfaction from my plight that I focused only on the positive aspects of the situation.

I placed the letter with others that would go out whenever someone made a trip to town. Knowing Aunt Phoebe, I expected no reply but felt better having discharged that obligation.

The speed with which news traveled among the widely scattered inhabitants of the territory never ceased to amaze me. No sooner had I announced my intention to remain than a trickle of would-be suitors began showing up on the Bradley doorstep.

In the weeks that followed, the trickle became a steady stream. I was puzzled at first, then amused, and finally driven to seek Abby's counsel.

"What have I done to make myself fair game?" I cried in frustration. "Abby, I promise you, I have never given any of them an indication that their attentions would be welcome. But just yesterday a total stranger rode in out of nowhere and asked me to marry him! When I turned him down, he just shrugged and rode off again. What am I to do?"

Abby pushed herself higher on her pillows and managed a weak chuckle. Her strength seemed to diminish a fraction with each passing day, but her good humor and interest in events at the ranch never wavered. The crisp fall air brought a tinge of color to her cheeks, and she looked at me now with a hint of the old sparkle dancing in her eyes.

"Why, Judith, what you've done is very serious," she said, attempting to sound stern. "You've become a permanent resident. An attractive, single, *female* resident. It's started every one of those lonely cowboys thinking how good it would be to come home to a wife and a place of his own.

"In a way," she said, laughing softly, "you really can't blame them. I guess they feel there's no harm in trying."

She became suddenly grave. "None of them has tried to force their attentions beyond decent limits, have they?"

"No," I admitted. "I have to give them credit for that. Nearly all of them have given up after the first 'no.' And the rest have gotten it through their heads after two or three tries . . . all except Shorty."

"Shorty! I should have guessed."

"I can't go anywhere or do anything without that man popping up. Just yesterday, the children and I were out walking. I would have sworn there wasn't anyone but the three of us around, but all of a sudden, there he was, all big soulful eyes and deep sighs, come to 'walk with us a ways.' Is this going to go on until I've exhausted every single man in the territory?"

"Well, there is one thing you could do."

"What?" I asked eagerly.

"You could take one of them up on his offer."

"Oh, Abby! I thought you were serious."

"I am. You're not planning to stay single all your life, are you?"

"Of course not. It's just that . . . well, the right person hasn't asked me yet."

"I was afraid of that. I don't know why Jeff's dragging his feet so." She laughed at my expression. "Don't worry. You don't make it terribly obvious, if that's what you're afraid of. Sometimes we women are just quicker to read the signs, that's all. Don't forget that I fell in love with a Bradley man myself."

"Maybe it's more one-sided than I thought. Maybe there's someone else?" She averted her eyes, and my heart sank. "Abby, please! You've got to tell me. There is someone, isn't there?"

"No, dear," she said, meeting my eyes again. "At least, not now. It happened a long time ago, and I hadn't thought of it for some time."

"Please. Tell me anyway."

"I hate to. No," she added hastily, "not for the reason you think. A member of my family was involved, and I suppose I feel responsible.

"It was while we lived in Texas," she continued. "A distant cousin of mine came to visit. I hadn't seen Lorelei since we were children, and she had grown into the most beautiful woman I have ever seen. She had skin like fine porcelain, with dark curls and deep blue eyes, and a way about her that could make you feel you were the only other person on earth.

"Jeff was much younger then and was absolutely captivated by her. It was a whirlwind courtship, and I'd never seen Jeff in such a fever. He had plans to expand the ranch, add stock, build a house. He seemed to be everywhere at once. . . ." Her voice trailed off.

"What happened?"

Abby sighed. "She left. Just up and left one day. Charles told me later she laughed at Jeff, told him it was foolish to think she would consent to live in a barren wasteland where she couldn't have the social life she was accustomed to.

"Jeff was devastated. It was his first love, and he believed it would last forever, that Lorelei felt as deeply as he did. We were terribly worried about him, but time seemed to heal the wounds, and he has never referred to her again. But now . . ."

"Now?" I prompted.

"I wonder if he's afraid of being hurt again. This country is terribly different from what you've been used to, and he knows you have family in Missouri you can return to if you choose."

"Oh, no," I moaned. "If he only realized! I sometimes think that if I had to choose between an Indian raid and Aunt Phoebe,

I'd take a chance on the Indians. But even if things had been better back there, it's not home to me anymore. I can't explain it, but I feel I belong here, that I was made for this place. It's never seemed barren or desolate to me."

"Does Jeff know that?"

"I've barely been able to speak to him the last few weeks. He's spent so much time out on roundup, and when he is at home, I seldom see him, except at supper. It's hardly the place to start that kind of conversation, with Charles and the children there, too. It's almost as though —" Sudden panic gripped me. "Abby, you don't think he's changed his mind, do you? That he's avoiding me?"

Abby laughed softly. "I don't think you need to worry about him changing his mind. As to avoiding you, he may need time to realize you won't change your mind and leave. Can you be very patient, if need be?"

"I can wait as long as it takes as long as I know he cares for me!" The heavy weight that had oppressed me lifted, and I felt light, free, and capable of all patience. "Now if I can just convince Shorty I'm not refusing everyone else to leave the way clear for him!"

We both laughed, and I went off to collect the children for their lessons with a lighter heart than I'd had for many a day.

Both Lizzie and Willie had bright, inquiring minds, and with the help of books I chose from Charles's library, I was trying to channel their curiosity in a more acceptable direction. Although I had no training as a teacher, I felt pleased with their progress.

We were sitting on the porch, reading aloud from *Ivanhoe*, when the Reverend Carver drove up in a rented buggy. I stood and went to greet him, assuming he had come to call on Abby. It was rather late for that, I thought peevishly, as he had not been to the ranch before in all the time he had been in the territory.

The Reverend Carver had been the topic of many a puzzled conversation among us. He had indeed stayed on, "to bring light into our dark corner of the world," as he put it, but his idea of being a shepherd seemed to stop at preaching a lukewarm sermon once a week on the goodness of man and the ills of society.

He turned a deaf ear to complaints that he ignored the sick and ailing of his flock. Attendance at the Sunday services had dropped to a pitifully low level.

Jake and the other cowboys had their fill early in the minister's tenure. Once, during a time of sharing testimonies, Shorty stood up and announced he wished to speak.

"Preacher," he drawled, "it seems you do a powerful lot of talking about bein' good and kind to one another, and that's all well and good. But me and the boys have been comin' to hear you for three weeks now, and you haven't said anything different from one time to the next. I've never even heard you mention the Good Book.

"Beggin' the pardon of everyone here, but if this is all there is to your brand of religion, I guess the boys and me can save ourselves the trip to town and talk to each other about how good we all are."

And with that, he, Neil, and two other men stalked out, leaving the congregation and the Reverend Carver in stunned silence. Even the Bradleys and I had not attended a service in several weeks. I spent much time reading my Bible, finding in it the guiding truths the Reverend Carver's sermons lacked. And now, after all these months, he came to call.

I said a quick "good day" to him and turned to lead him through the house to see Abby. I was anxious to get back to Lizzie and Willie and their reading lesson.

To my surprise, he laid his hand on my arm and whispered, "Please, may I speak with you alone?"

Annoyed at the delay, I showed him to a seat in the parlor, hoping Charles, Vera, anyone would come along to take over. His face shone with beads of perspiration, and his hands shook. I wondered if he were becoming ill himself. I was about to offer him a drink of water when he spoke.

"Miss Alder." He cleared his throat nervously. "Judith. I . . . I hardly know how to begin."

It was all I could do to keep from tapping my foot impatiently. This was usually a busy area of the house. Why didn't someone come?

"I find great gratification in my work here," he went on. "But some days the time does lie heavy on my hands, and I begin to think."

I thought to myself that if he would spend more time visiting the sick and tending to other pastoral duties, he would have less of it on his hands.

"A man gets lonely, Judith," he said, and I realized with a sick feeling where this conversation was heading. "He begins to realize his need for a companion, someone to share the lonely times, the bleak moments, as well as the joys of success."

"You hardly paint a happy picture of married life," I said tartly. To my relief, I heard footsteps approaching from the hallway. Rescue was at hand!

"Your smile, your sweet disposition, all lead me to believe you would make an ideal companion."

Hurry, I willed whoever was beyond the door. My heart leaped when it opened and Jeff stood framed in the doorway. He opened his mouth to speak, but at that moment, the Reverend Carver flung himself on his knees before me and cried, "Judith, I am asking you to be my wife."

The three of us remained frozen for what seemed an eternity. Jeff finally broke the silence.

"Excuse me," he said. "I seem to be interrupting." He turned on his heel and was gone.

"Jeff, wait!" I cried, utterly ignoring the Reverend Carver, who still knelt on the floor. I ran to the doorway, but Jeff's long strides had already carried him out of sight. I turned in exasperation to find my suitor standing immediately behind me, hands clasped in pleading.

"Judith, please. What is your answer?"

"My answer is no!" It came out sharper

than I had intended, but I was too vexed to care.

"I see." He drew himself up with far more dignity than he had shown up to now. "I have tried to bestow upon you the greatest honor a man can give to a woman. You have refused me most abruptly. May I hope that, after you have had time to give the idea due consideration, you may change your mind?"

"Please," I said, fighting to keep my temper in check. "I appreciate your kind proposal, but you must accept my answer as final."

"Very well," he said stiffly. "Then I will not trouble you again." He stopped at the door and turned. "Judith, this was intended as much for your good as for mine. Considering the . . . unorthodox manner of your arrival here, do you think you can ever truly be accepted by the people? Come away with me, and we'll start a new life together."

My temper was slipping its restraints. "You're quite mistaken about my acceptance here. The Bradleys opened their home freely and have entrusted their children's care to me. Surely they wouldn't do that for anyone whose morals might be suspect.

"Any other notions about my respectability come from the fevered imagination of Lucia Styles. I am not concerned about her malicious gossip, and I beg you not to be, either."

His lips tightened, and he closed the door behind him with more force than was strictly necessary. I breathed a sigh of relief and ran to look for Jeff. Not finding him in the house, I hurried outdoors toward the corral, where I found Jake leaning against the rail.

"You wouldn't be lookin' for Jeff now, would you?" he asked, a twinkle in his eye.

"Have you seen him, Jake? Where is he?"

"He came stormin' out of the house a few minutes ago, threw a saddle and some gear on his horse, and said he was going to check the stock up on the north range. Said he'd be back in about a week."

"A week!"

"Uh-huh. Kept mutterin' something about women while he was gettin' ready. Any idea what he meant?" he asked, with an air of innocence a child could have seen through.

I was beyond answering. I turned and scanned the horizon. Jeff must have ridden like the wind; the gently rolling hills held no sign of him.

A week to live through before I could see him and explain. A week for him to imagine all sorts of mistaken situations. I forced one foot in front of the other and made my way back to the front porch to finish the interrupted lesson.

"Did the minister come to see Mama?" Lizzie asked.

"Why was he so mad when he left?" Willie wondered. "He jumped in his rig and took off like he was gonna run that horse to death."

"He did seem upset, didn't he?" I murmured. "Let's see, what page were we on?"

"I'll bet he didn't come to see Mama at all," Lizzie said. "He wasn't here long enough for a real visit. And besides, Mama doesn't make people mad like that."

"Here we are," I announced brightly. "Page thirty-eight. Lizzie, I believe it was your turn to read."

"You're right," Willie said, as though I weren't there. "Mama doesn't make anybody mad." He eyed me speculatively. "But *she* does."

"I . . . I what?"

"Make people mad," Willie answered solemnly. "I heard Jake say he never saw any woman in his life that got people stirred up more."

"Willie!" scolded his sister. "You're not supposed to say things like that."

"But it's true, Lizzie! You know it's true. Like when you told Shorty he ought to ask her to marry him —"

"Willie, don't," Lizzie warned.

"— and he did, and she said she wouldn't."

"Willie!" Lizzie shrilled.

"Remember how mad he was before you told him he ought to keep trying and not give up?"

"Willieee!" Lizzie screeched, leaping upon her brother and trying to cover his mouth with her hands.

By this time, I had recovered sufficiently to pry them apart, and the three of us stood looking at one another.

"Lizzie," I panted, "you didn't really tell Shorty to . . . to . . ."

"Sure she did," Willie bragged. This time Lizzie silenced him with a look.

"But why?"

"Well," she said reluctantly, "Vera said you looked sad one day, and she thought it was because you were pining for someone. So I thought if you got married, you'd be able to quit pining and be happy."

"I see. Uh, Lizzie, you didn't say this

kind of thing to anyone besides Shorty, did you?"

"Well . . ."

"Oh, she told lots of people," put in the helpful Willie. "Lots and lots. *Lots* and *lots* and . . ." Catching sight of both our faces, he trailed off. "We just didn't want you to pine," he mumbled.

"Children," I said, "our lesson is over for today. Go to the kitchen and see what Vera can find for you." They scampered off in relief, and I sagged limply against the porch rail.

Chapter 10

Much to my surprise, the week flew by in spite of Jeff's absence. I had fully expected to "pine," as Lizzie put it, worrying about his frame of mind. Instead, the week was so full of activity that I had little time to dwell on my problem.

Charles had given a steer to an old settler and his wife in the next valley. The man had broken his leg on a hunting trip and found himself laid up for weeks, unable to work or hunt. Pride kept the couple from asking for help, and by the time one of the Double B cowboys noticed their plight, they were subsisting mostly on apples from their orchard.

In gratitude, they sent over a wagon load of apples, and Vera and I fell heir to the task of putting them up.

We peeled and cored and sliced all week long. Some went in the canning kettle to be added to the glistening rows of jars already lining the pantry shelves. Others,

Vera baked into pies.

The smell of their baking brought more than one cowboy to the kitchen, where Vera had them sweep the floor, carry out ashes, or bring in wood for the stove before she served them a generous helping.

"Baking takes extra time," she said, grinning, "but this way we have a lot of chores taken off our hands."

I laughed and agreed that it wasn't a bad trade.

Most of the apples were cored and sliced and the slices strung to hang over the woodstove to dry. These would keep almost indefinitely and could be taken along by the men when they rode out on the range or used by Vera for baking as the winter progressed.

Lessons were suspended for the time being; Lizzie and Willie sat on low stools in the kitchen and strung the slices as we cut them. I was touched to see how seriously they took the task, carefully spacing the rounds so they didn't touch and the air could move freely around them.

Willie showed impressive skill, going through his bowl of slices nearly twice as quickly as his sister. I noticed, though, that we didn't hang his strings over the stove any more often. I was about to comment on this when he let out a horrible groan.

I looked to see what was wrong. He had turned a light shade of green and was doubled over, clutching his stomach.

"Willie!" I cried, kneeling beside him. "What's wrong?"

"Oooh, it hurts. It hurts!" was all he could say before he went off into a series of pathetic moans.

Vera felt his forehead. "He's cold and clammy," she told me. "No fever. Help me get him to bed."

Between us, we carried him to his room. By the time Vera turned down the covers on his bed, beads of perspiration stood out on his forehead.

We laid him between the sheets, still moaning, and I found I was trembling almost as much as Willie.

"What is it, Vera? Do you know?" Memories of a child back in Missouri whose appendix had ruptured rushed into my mind, and the remembrance of the tragic consequences chilled me.

"I have an idea," she said. "You go on back and tend to Lizzie. She looked almost as scared as you do."

I marveled at her calm as I ran back to the kitchen where Lizzie sat, white faced. I sat in the big rocker and held out my arms, and she came readily. We took comfort in each other's presence as we rocked silently, waiting. I was debating whether or not to disturb Abby with the news when Vera appeared in the doorway.

"Is it serious? Should we call his parents?"

"How's my brother?" Our words tumbled over one another as we scrambled out of the rocker.

Vera settled herself comfortably in her chair and mopped her forehead before she spoke. "Willie's just fine," she said.

"But his stomach . . . I'm sure he was really in pain. . . ."

"Oh, he was in pain, right enough," she agreed as she picked up her paring knife and another bowl of apples.

"Vera!" I cried in exasperation. I was astonished to hear her chuckle.

"Now, didn't you notice how fast Willie strung those apples?"

"Yes, but what —"

"And didn't you think it was peculiar that with all that speed, he didn't finish any more strings than Lizzie?"

"Yes, I wondered about it. But what does that have to do with it?"

"That little scamp was eating a slice for every one he strung." She grinned. "He must have popped one in his mouth whenever he figured we weren't looking."

I looked at the strings festooned over the stove. Half of them were Willie's, and to eat that many apples at once . . . "Good heavens! Why, that would . . ."

"Uh-huh. Young Master Willie had a good old-fashioned bellyache."

I laughed in relief. "But you're sure he's going to be all right?"

"Let's just say that nature has taken its course," she said drily. "He'll feel a mite puny the rest of the day, but by morning he'll be looking for new mischief to get into."

"Thank goodness." We settled back into our routine. Lizzie seemed rather subdued, which could have been expected after a scare like that. But I had noticed that many of her quiet spells were followed by some type of prank, and I wondered what we might be in for next.

Vera broke into my reverie. "Have you decided how you'll decorate your box?" she asked.

"What box?"

Her hands flew to her face. "Mercy! Don't tell me I clean forgot to tell you?"

"Tell me what?" I asked, bewildered.

"About the box supper social this week."

She sighed. “I must be getting old. I didn’t say a word about it, did I?”

“I guess not. I’m still not sure what we’re talking about.”

“There’s to be a get-together in town next Saturday night to raise money for a school. People will be coming in from all over this part of the territory.”

“Oh. That sounds nice.”

“Honey, haven’t you ever been to a box supper?”

“No,” I admitted. “Are we going to this one?”

“You’d better smile, we’re going! All of us except Charles and Abby and the children. And you’ll be a little more excited once you hear what it’s all about.”

“All right.” I laughed. “Satisfy my curiosity. You’ve certainly stirred it up.”

Vera took her time removing the core from the apple she was working on. “Well,” she began, “all the single ladies cook up the best supper they can and pack it in a box. Then they decorate their boxes real fancy and take them along to the supper.

“When it’s time to eat, the men bid on the boxes. The highest bid gets the box, the supper, *and* the company of the lady that fixed it.”

“You mean they auction them? But how

do they know whose box they're bidding for?"

"It's all supposed to be a secret," she said. "And some of the fellows don't care so much about whose it is as getting a good home-cooked supper and some female companionship while they're eating.

"But the ones who really want to sit with a certain young lady usually have some way of finding out ahead of time." She eyed me slyly. "Might be worth your while."

I shot her a sharp glance. "What is that supposed to mean?"

"Nothing," she replied airily. "Just that when a man and a woman are having trouble getting off on the right foot, a long conversation over a good meal sure can't hurt."

I bit off a tart reply and peeled apples with fervor, hoping Vera would think the flush I could feel on my face was due to the heat of the stove. She wouldn't be fooled for a minute, though. She seemed to have a sixth sense when it came to human relationships.

Well, why not take her advice? The way to a man's heart might not really be through his stomach, but it might help to pave the way.

The more I thought about it, the more my spirits rose. Jeff's initial reaction to the scene he witnessed with the Reverend Carver was understandable, but he'd had nearly a week to think about it. Granted, he hadn't heard my refusal, but surely he realized I wouldn't accept.

If he returned on time, he should be home tomorrow. I built up the scene in my mind. I would go to meet him and simply explain what had happened. He would have regained his good humor during his week away, and we would laugh together over the incident.

With the ice thus broken, the box supper two days later would give us the perfect opportunity to iron things out. Maybe reach some kind of understanding. Maybe even . . . I took a firm hold on my soaring imagination before I became positively giddy. There would be a lot of planning to do over the next few days — what dress to wear, what food to prepare — but it would all be worth it in the end. Vera was right, I was sure. It would all work out.

That evening I sat on the porch, watching a harvest moon rise above the hills. Its brightness washed the countryside with a silver glow. It was a pity, I thought, that its beauty would be waning by the night of the social. I consoled myself by thinking of Jeff lying in his bedroll under the stars, staring at the same moon. Was he thinking of me at this moment?

Next morning, I took special pains with my appearance before hurrying to help Vera finish the last batch of apples. Both the children worked with us again, Willie having recovered according to Vera's prediction. I noticed that today he conscientiously strung every slice. It would be quite some time, I suspected, before he felt tempted to gorge on apples again.

With the last of the strings hung over the stove, I put the children through their lessons at a rapid pace and sent them, protesting, to straighten their rooms. I gathered up some mending and stationed myself on the porch, where I could watch the horizon. Today was the day.

The sun had nearly reached its peak when a shout from one of the stablehands drew my attention to a rider coming from the north. I leaned against the porch rail to watch, turning over in my mind exactly what I would say. It was silly to let silence come between us when a few words of explanation could have smoothed the way.

The rider drew closer, and as he neared the bunkhouse, I could see that it was Jeff.

Just the sight of him astride his mount made me catch my breath with love and pride. He reined in his horse and swung down from the saddle.

I drew a deep breath and started toward the stable to greet him. Jeff had his hat off now and was mopping his brow. The boy who came to take his horse looked past me and gestured toward the road. I glanced over my shoulder and saw a buggy coming. It looked like the Styleses'.

I nearly laughed out loud. Let Lucia Styles come, disapproving glares and all. This was my moment, my turning point. All the busybodies in the world couldn't take it from me.

Following the gesture, Jeff, too, had seen the buggy, but now his eyes were focused on me. I stopped under a cottonwood and waited for him, trying to remain calm. He smiled, and I saw only warmth and tenderness in his glance. It was just as I had imagined; soon we would be laughing over the incident together.

I stretched out my hands to him. "I'm glad you're back. There's something I want to explain." My hands remained suspended in the air as he stood stock-still in front of me, his gaze riveted on a point somewhere over my shoulder.

Turning to locate the distraction, I found the buggy had drawn up behind us. It was indeed the Styleses' buggy, but alighting from it was the most beautiful creature I had ever seen. Finely chiseled features, raven hair, and a porcelain complexion combined to give an impression of exquisite loveliness and fragility.

She smiled radiantly. "Jefferson, dear. It's been so long."

I wheeled around to face Jeff. He gaped at the newcomer as though seeing a ghost and choked out one word: "Lorelei!"

Chapter 11

I stared at the array of frills spread across my bed: scraps of fabric and colored paper, bits of lace, ribbons, and buttons of assorted sizes, all donated by Vera to decorate my box. I moved different items around in various combinations without finding one that suited me. But then, nothing seemed to please me lately.

The entire household felt the strain of the last two days. Lorelei, it seemed, heard of Abby's illness through the family grapevine and took it upon herself to come out to "care for dear cousin Abby through these last trying days."

My own feeling was that the days hadn't been nearly so trying before Lorelei arrived, but I took care to hold my tongue. She was, after all, a member of the family.

She had taken up residence in the room next to Abby's to be available whenever she was needed. I couldn't help noticing that Abby's periods of rest came more frequently and lasted longer, and I wondered whether her condition was worsening or if this was her only means of gaining some moments of privacy.

Whatever the case, it gave Lorelei ample time to explore the ranch, in Jeff's company, more often than not. During the children's lessons on the porch, we often saw them strolling arm in arm.

Lizzie and Willie didn't seem to be any happier about her coming than I was. She made overtures to them both on the day of her arrival but soon retreated under their sullen glares. I chided them for their lack of courtesy, but the rebuke was halfhearted on my part, and they seemed to sense it.

My own conversations with her had been as brief as I could politely manage. I could see she was curious about me. She approached me shortly before supper on her first evening at the ranch.

"I can't tell you what a relief it is to see that the children are being cared for properly," she said with a bright smile. "That was worrying my poor mother to death. And here they are with a regular . . . governess, would you call yourself? What an asset you must be! Did Charles advertise back east?"

Knowing full well by then that she met

Lucia Styles upon her arrival in Three Forks and had prevailed upon her for a ride to the ranch, I confined my answer to a simple no. She would have already heard the Styleses' version of my arrival, and I had no intention of trying to defend myself.

"Jefferson has told me what a help you are with the little dears." She lowered her voice to a confidential tone. "Jefferson and I are old, old friends, you know."

I clenched my teeth and displayed them in what I hoped would be convincing as a smile. Vera came to call us for supper at that moment.

"Well, dear," Lorelei said, "I'll see you after supper, and we'll have a cozy little chat." She looked surprised when I followed her to the dining room. "Oh, do you eat here with the family? Why, how very . . . democratic!" And with a flash of dazzling white teeth, she swirled away to her seat.

Despite the addition of a guest, dinner that night was not a festive event. The children stared steadfastly at their plates. Charles, usually the perfect host, made several attempts at conversation, then trailed off, at a loss for words. Jeff was apparently still in shock from her unexpected arrival and alternated between staring at Lorelei and pushing food aimlessly about on his plate. My appetite, too, had vanished.

Only Lorelei seemed unaware of the lack of conviviality. She chattered on and on about her journey by train and stagecoach, about the relatives in Virginia, and how wonderful it was to be with dear Charles and Abby and Jefferson.

By the time dessert was ready to be served, I pleaded a headache and went to my room.

Things continued in much the same fashion over the next two days, with Charles struggling to be courteous, Jeff in a daze, and Lorelei either attending Abby or attaching herself to Jeff.

"Like a . . . a leech," I complained bitterly to Vera on the morning of the box supper. Deprived of Abby's counsel, I turned to Vera with my doubts and frustrations. Knowing she was well aware of my feelings for Jeff, it had been a relief to unburden myself to her.

"Just when I thought it was all working out, she comes along and everything falls apart."

"Well, for heaven's sake, girl," Vera snapped. "If something's worth having, it's worth fighting for, isn't it? She's with Abby most of the time, isn't she? Get out there when you've got a chance and talk to the man."

"It's not that easy. He's away from the house so much of the day, and when he is around, Lorelei's free and needs him as an escort." I slumped miserably against the kitchen counter. "And what would I say now, anyway? 'Make up your mind, Jeff, and choose between us?' I couldn't do that."

Vera sniffed. "I didn't say it was going to be easy. Nothing worth having ever is. All I know is, if I cared about someone as much as you care about Jeff Bradley, you can bet I'd be willing to put up a fight!"

I had to smile at the thought of Lorelei and me dueling over Jeff in the courtyard. But Vera's talk had its effect. I didn't have to resort to punching and jabbing, but neither did I have to crawl away like a whipped pup, handing Lorelei the victory by default. There were more ways to win a fight than with a clenched fist.

Under Vera's guidance, I soon had an apple pie in the oven, with biscuits to follow. Crispy fried chicken, potatoes, and gravy would complete the meal, which Vera assured me was Jeff's favorite.

Lorelei came to the kitchen in the afternoon while Vera was finishing her own box supper, to fix, as she put it, "some fancy sandwiches for that quaint little social." We watched in astonishment while she cut bread into elaborate shapes and filled the sandwiches with bits of ham.

I had been on the ranch long enough to know what a hard day's work did for a man's appetite. Any one of the cowboys could easily have devoured the entirety of Lorelei's meal without batting an eye, then looked around for the main course. I felt a stab of sympathy for her and hoped whoever bought her supper would be gentleman enough not to complain too loudly.

Watching Lorelei's lovely form while she worked at the counter, I was assailed by a flood of doubt. I looked upon her as an interloper, but what if Jeff honestly did prefer her to me? He loved her once; had he really gotten over it, as Abby thought?

Now the time had come to decorate my box, and I was busy wrestling with my feelings. "All right," I said aloud. "Suppose the worst happens. Do you love him enough to want him to be happy? Enough to be glad to let him go to Lorelei if that's what he truly wants?"

I did, I realized with a mixture of pain

and relief. I had done nothing to be ashamed of in loving him. I would do nothing now to embarrass or hurt him in any way. It was his choice; he would have to make up his own mind.

I picked up a length of red ribbon. A milliner had once shown me how to fashion a rose out of ribbon. Did I still remember how? A fold, a few twists, and while the end result wasn't of professional quality, it was at least recognizable. Jeff and Charles had mentioned once how much they missed the roses that grew at their Texas ranch. I would give him a garden of roses.

I twisted ribbon after ribbon, forming roses of varied sizes and hues, enough to nearly cover the top of my box. I wrapped the box in soft green cloth as the base of my "garden," then carefully fastened the roses to it. Lizzie and Willie burst through the door when I was nearly finished.

"Oh, it's beautiful!" Lizzie cried, and I basked in the warmth of her praise.

"Green, with flowers," muttered Willie to himself, as if committing it to memory.

"We were hoping you had it finished," Lizzie said.

"Yeah," said Willie, " 'cause someone's been asking us what it looked — ow!" He broke off when a well-aimed kick caught him on the shin.

"Well, now you've seen it. But you know," I added virtuously, "that no one is supposed to know who made which box."

"We know," Lizzie agreed cheerfully. "And we wouldn't tell . . . not just anybody, anyway!"

I hugged myself in delight when they left, giggling. "Not just anybody," indeed! I hadn't imagined his feelings for me, after all. Of course Lorelei's coming had stunned him; that was only natural. And it was just as natural that he could not avoid her. After all, she was a guest at the ranch, and Jeff felt obliged to be courteous.

But tonight — tonight when the bidding was going on for the supposedly anonymous suppers — it could hardly be considered neglect of Lorelei to fail to bid on hers. I fastened the last few ribbon roses to the box with tender care. It did look lovely, if I said so myself.

I realized with a shock that I had spent so much time preparing the box that I barely had enough time to get myself ready.

The dress I had chosen was pale blue with a tight bodice and puffy sleeves. It seemed too lovely to wear before, even to church, and I wondered about the wisdom of subjecting it to the long wagon ride into town. But this night, at least, I was determined to shine.

The dress fit as though made for me, and for the hundredth time I blessed Abby for her generosity. She must have looked stunning in this dress. I turned to study myself in the mirror. Excitement and the mounting anticipation brought a pink flush to my cheeks and an expectant sparkle to my eyes. I smoothed a stray wisp of hair into place and grinned at the girl in the glass.

Vera found a dark blue cloak for me to use as a wrap, and I was glad of its warmth when I stepped out to the waiting wagon. The rays of the late afternoon sun didn't do a thing to combat the crisp chill. Autumn was definitely in the air.

Vera waited just outside the kitchen door. "Here, give me your box before anybody sees it," she said. She set it carefully inside a covered basket next to two other boxes of similar size. One was wrapped in calico, the other in a cloth of delicate blue with a wide ruffle of lace around the edge and a large velvet bow on the top. It wasn't difficult to decide which box was whose.

"You did a nice job." She smiled approvingly. “The roses were a nice touch.” She gave me a sly wink as she closed the basket. I laughed happily, letting the mood of the evening take over.

Shorty and Neil placed a box at the end of the wagon for us to use as a step and stood ready to assist us as we climbed in. Shorty was wearing his cologne again. The aroma wafted over us as he helped me step to the wagon bed, and I hoped it would not cling to my hair or clothes.

Vera shook off their hands and stepped up herself, carefully balancing the basket as she did so. Neil reached out to take it from her, but she slapped his hand away.

“Keep those hands to yourself,” she snapped. “You’re just dying to lift that lid and see how those boxes are done up. But you’re just going to have to wait your turn like everyone else!”

Shorty hooted at Neil’s discomfiture until Vera wheeled toward him and said, “And you, you’ll do us all a favor if you’ll stay downwind.”

I sat on one of the blankets that had been laid over fluffy piles of straw, carefully smoothing my skirts to avoid as many wrinkles as possible. Vera sat opposite, guarding her basket jealously.

A strangling noise from Shorty made us

turn. He and Neil were gaping at the vision of loveliness framed in the doorway. Lorelei had a knack for making an entrance a grand event. She had only to stand, as she did now, looking helpless and appealing, and every man in the vicinity would fall all over himself to go to her aid.

Shorty and Neil sprang forward, each trying to be the first to reach her. They collided, bounced apart, and stumbled to her side together.

"Looks like a tie," Vera muttered.

Lorelei appeared to regard it as such, for she favored each contender with one of her brilliant smiles and allowed each of them to tuck one of her dainty hands in the crook of his arm. They led her to the wagon in state, the picture of well-trained footmen, and helped her tenderly into the wagon as though she might break.

"I never saw anything like it," Vera said to me in a low voice. "All she has to do is stand there." We watched, fascinated, while she seated herself upon the straw as though it were a throne. She smiled graciously at her courtiers, dismissing them, and turned to us.

Evidently, Lorelei was not immune to the excitement of the evening, for she seemed as inclined to giggle and chatter as a schoolgirl.

"Isn't this quaint?" she gushed. "It'll be such fun to tell everybody back home about it. Imagine . . . taking a chance on spending the evening with a total stranger!" She shivered in delicious anticipation.

"Appears to me that it's the men who are taking the risk," Vera said drily. "They're buying two pigs in a poke — the company and the meal."

"Why, what an unflattering comparison, Vera dear!" Lorelei laughed gaily.

Vera opened her mouth as if to make a retort, and I was relieved when Jake's sudden arrival interrupted them. "Your driver at your service, ladies," he announced grandly. "And there's no one who'll be driving any lovelier ladies to the supper."

"I'm inclined to agree," said Jeff, stepping out of the doorway.

"Jefferson!" Lorelei exclaimed. "Don't you look fine!" He stood tall and straight in his black frock coat and striped pants.

"Thank you," he said, stepping easily into the wagon and settling himself between us. "May I return the compliment?" While Lorelei fluttered happily, he turned to me and said softly, "You look lovely tonight, Judith." His smile was like a caress. I found myself suddenly unable to speak, but smiled back at him with my heart in my eyes.

Jake stepped nimbly to the seat, shook out the reins with a flourish, and we were off. Neil and Shorty mounted their horses and rode beside the wagon. The evening's excitement was infectious, and good-natured banter flew back and forth between the wagon and the riders. Even Neil shook off some of his shyness and ventured an occasional comment.

Lorelei dominated the conversation, batting her eyes first at one cowboy, then another, archly accusing all the men of trying to find out which basket belonged to which girl.

Shorty's and Neil's mounts proved unexpectedly susceptible to injury, Neil's bruising its foot on a stone and Shorty's acquiring a limp perceptible only to Shorty himself.

Both tied their horses to the tailgate and climbed into the now crowded wagon. As the only available space was along Vera's side, it placed both of them opposite Lorelei, which seemed to satisfy them admirably.

Vera grumbled and held on to the basket. Jake remarked loudly that there was plenty of room next to him on the seat, but no one seemed to pay any attention.

With Lorelei holding court and the cowboys eagerly competing for her attention, the rest of us were left to amuse ourselves. This suited me well enough; it was pleasant just to sit close to Jeff without having to say anything.

The sun slipped behind the mountains and there was a chill in the air. I drew my cloak around me and shivered.

"Cold?" Jeff reached around me to tuck a blanket about my shoulders.

At that moment, one of the rear wheels hit a hole, and the wagon lurched violently. I was thrown back against Jeff, whose arm tightened protectively around me. It took a moment to recover my balance sufficiently to right myself. Recovering my composure took longer. Fortunately, everyone else had been similarly thrown about, and no one seemed to notice.

"I'm sorry," I whispered, dismayed to find my breath coming in little gasps.

"I'm not," he said quietly. His smile had faded, and he looked at me intently in the twilight.

We said nothing more during the ride into town, but that moment hung between us like a promise.

Chapter 12

Lights spilled out of the windows of the warehouse and painted yellow squares on the darkened street. Jake let us out at the door and went to find a place to leave the wagon.

We moved through a swirling throng of gaily laughing people, only a few of whom I recognized. I followed Vera, and we threaded our way to a long table already covered with decorated boxes. I looked them over quickly, but none resembled my "rose garden." My breath whooshed out in a sigh of relief. There shouldn't be any doubt as to which was mine.

Vera handed her basket to one of the women presiding over the table, and we retired to a corner, out of the crush.

"I had no idea there were this many people to be found around here," I said, panting slightly.

Vera produced a handkerchief from her sleeve and dabbed at her forehead.

"They've come for miles in all directions. Anything like this happens so seldom that it brings them right out of the woodwork. Those who aren't in on the auction brought potluck suppers and will donate money, anyway. And the thought of having a school and a good teacher for their youngsters — the bidding ought to go high tonight."

I looked at the children scampering around the room and felt a momentary pang of regret for Lizzie and Willie. How they would have loved playing with them! But, no, they needed a quiet evening alone with their parents even more. There had been little enough time for them as a family lately.

A tall, lean man stood up on a platform behind the long table and tried vainly to get the crowd's attention. He called, he whistled, he clapped his hands, but even though I was watching him, I couldn't hear him over the din.

Finally, a husky, square-shouldered fellow motioned him off the platform, mounted it himself, and let out a screeching war whoop. The effect was almost miraculous. All eyes turned toward the man, who bowed, stepped down with a grin, and pushed the tall man back up again. "They're all yours, Sam," he announced.

"All right, folks," said the one called Sam. "It's about time we got started. Ladies, please have a seat on the benches over there along the wall. Gentlemen, you line up here on this side so you can all see what you'll be bidding on. I'm your auctioneer for the evening, and I hope you men all brought good appetites and full wallets so we can raise plenty of money for the new school!"

A cheer rose and died away as we all moved to find our places. I had begun to feel guilty about leaving Lorelei to her own devices, but when we made our way toward the benches lining the far wall, I saw her talking animatedly to a group of young men. Even here, she was the undisputed belle of the ball.

Her admirers escorted her to one of the benches and left, reluctantly, I thought. I sat between her and Vera and scanned the group of men opposite. Jeff leaned comfortably against the wall. His eyes met mine and a smile lit his face.

"Isn't this exciting?" Lorelei whispered delightedly. I nodded, in complete agreement with her for once.

"Ladies and gentlemen," intoned the

auctioneer, "the auction will now begin!" He held up a box covered with yellow paper cutouts of the moon and stars. "What am I bid for this box, which promises to contain a heavenly feast?"

A ripple of nervous laughter swept the room, but no one seemed inclined to open the bidding.

"Come, come," the auctioneer chided. "No need to be shy, folks. Let's start the bidding at twenty-five cents. Who'll be first?"

A hand went up across the room. "That's more like it! Now do I hear thirty cents? Thirty cents for the new schoolhouse?"

"I'll bid thirty."

"Thirty-five."

The bidding began to grow more spirited, and a final bid of fifty-five cents brought the auctioneer's gavel crashing down on the table.

"Sold!" he cried. "To Eb Winters for fifty-five cents. Step right up, Eb. Claim your dinner and your partner."

Eb Winters, a tall, gangly youth who looked to be barely out of his teens, moved forward, grinning sheepishly. He handed over his money amid good-natured catcalls, took his box, and turned to look hopefully for his dinner partner.

A pleasant-faced woman of about fifty stepped out of the crowd and went to join him. Eb made an obvious effort to control his disappointment and escorted his companion to a table with dignity.

I began to wonder just how enjoyable the evening would be for most of the participants. My concern must have shown on my face, for Vera patted me on the knee and said, "Don't worry, honey. She's one of the best cooks around. By the time he eats his fill and she gets finished mothering him, he'll feel like he got more than his money's worth."

Sure enough, Eb was tucking into his supper as though he hadn't eaten for a month. His partner watched with pleasure, smiling maternally and urging him to take even more. Looking at it from Vera's point of view, it made sense. In fact, judging from the crowd's reaction, a good deal of the fun was in the unlikely matches that occurred.

More of the tables were filling up as the boxes went to their various buyers. I became interested in watching the reactions of the girls and women around me as the tension mounted as to whose box would be offered next.

The auctioneer held aloft a box wrapped only in brown paper, with birds drawn on it. It was easy enough to see that it belonged to a young girl sitting back near the wall by the wave of crimson that spread over her face. The bidding started slowly, to the girl's obvious embarrassment.

A flurry of activity on the other side of the room caught my eye. A boy of about the same age as the girl was sidling along the wall, stopping first at one man, then the next. Some of the men slipped something from their pockets into the boy's hand, while others shook their heads. The boy reached the end of the line and hurriedly examined his collection.

"Forty cents," said the auctioneer. "Are there no more bids? Going once . . . going twice . . ."

"I bid seventy-eight cents!" cried the boy. The auctioneer swept his gavel down, and the girl, still blushing, walked away with her hero.

There were now no more than half a dozen suppers on the auction table, Vera's, Lorelei's, and mine among them. The men still waiting to bid began to take special notice of the boxes being presented.

Once Jeff offered a bid on one of the suppers, and my heart stopped. Again Vera reassured me. "See the 'RT' down in the corner? Everybody knows that's Rose Taylor's box and she's sweet on Bill Carson. Bill doesn't want anyone else to have her, but he's one of the biggest skinflints you ever saw. Jeff just wanted to make him pay what the supper's worth, that's all."

As usual, Vera was right. After giving Jeff a baleful look, a glowering man with shaggy black hair made the final bid and led Rose away.

Vera's box was the next to go. She was calmer than I was as we watched the bidding mount. I wanted to cry out with pleasure when the gavel rang out on the final bid of a dollar. She squeezed my hand and gave me an encouraging wink. "It won't be long now," she whispered as she left.

And it wasn't. In no time at all, only two boxes remained — my garden of roses and Lorelei's lace-trimmed confection. I was glad now that most of the room was engaged in eating; the strain of waiting was bad enough without being the center of the whole group's attention.

Lorelei wore the look of a contented, cream-fed cat. She was actually enjoying the suspense, I realized. The whole thing couldn't be over soon enough for me.

The auctioneer paused dramatically and

made a show of deciding which box to pick up next. His hand moved from one to the other and back again before finally settling on mine.

He held the box under his nose and inhaled deeply. "Aaah," he sighed. "Gentlemen, I won't tell you what is in here, but I guarantee that if it tastes as delectable as it smells, it contains a meal fit for a king!" I felt pleased despite my nervousness, but I wished he would get on with it. I was interested in only one particular bidder.

My eyes sought out Jeff. He lounged casually against the wall, a slight smile on his face. I was glad that he, at least, could relax but did wish he would show a little more enthusiasm.

"Men," cried the auctioneer, "if you're hungry, you'd better wake up and bid. This is almost your last chance. Let's hear an opening bid."

"Twenty-five cents."

"Thirty."

"I'll go thirty-five."

Something was hurting my arm. I looked down to see Lorelei gripping it tightly with both hands. "Who do you think it will be?" She looked unaccountably anxious.

"The highest bidder, I suppose," I replied, trying to keep my voice steady. I laced my fingers tightly together and willed my hands to lay calmly in my lap, hoping no one would notice the white knuckles that betrayed my nervousness.

Now that the moment had come, I was assailed by sudden fears. What if something went wrong? But how could it, barring fire, flood, or imminent collapse of the roof? My lungs ached for air, and I realized I had been holding my breath.

"Forty-five cents," called out a cowboy.

"Sixty!" I recognized the voice as Shorty's. I started, then smiled shakily as I remembered Jeff's ploy with Bill Carson. Jeff would want to make a nice contribution to the school fund; evidently he was using Shorty to drive the price up.

"Seventy-five." I breathed a sigh of relief. Jeff had joined the bidding at last.

"Eighty-five," sang out the cowboy, getting into the spirit of things.

"One dollar." Jeff grinned.

Shorty looked irritated. He was playing his part well. He felt in one pocket, frowned, and explored the depths of the other. His face cleared. "I bid two dollars," he announced. We had everyone's attention now. A jump of a dollar in the bidding was unheard of.

"Two fifty," Jeff said.

The cowboy sat down resignedly. Silence fell, and the auctioneer raised his gavel. "Two fifty," he announced. "I have two fifty. Will anybody make it three?" He paused hopefully, scanning the men's faces. "Going once . . . going twice . . ."

"Three dollars!" shouted Shorty, his face as red as mine felt.

"Three dollars," echoed the auctioneer. Silence again.

"Going once . . ."

"Hurry, Jeff," I breathed.

"Going twice . . ."

"Please. Just get it over." I fidgeted, exasperated. This charade had gone on more than long enough to suit me.

"Sold!" The gavel rang out on the table. "Folks, let's hear it for Shorty Nelson, the highest bidder so far tonight!" Enthusiastic applause rocked the room. Lorelei gave my arm another squeeze.

Shorty swaggered to the table and counted out his money with a flourish. I sat in stunned disbelief. Could Jeff possibly have run out of money? He stood watching, grinning broadly. He didn't look at all like a man disappointed.

I rose woodenly and somehow got to Shorty's side. I didn't dare risk another look at Jeff.

How Shorty managed to get himself, the three-dollar supper, and me to a small table in a corner of the room, I never knew. The whole evening seemed like a bad dream. I had to make a determined effort in order to be aware of anything at all.

It struck me then that Shorty was fumbling with the wrapping on the box, and I roused myself to help him. It was hardly fair to him to be penalized for making such a gallant gesture. Three dollars, I knew, was the equivalent of several days' wages to the cowboys — hardly a sum to be dismissed lightly.

My fingers moved mechanically, trying to disturb the ribbon roses as little as possible. The room began to come back in focus again, and I realized that Lorelei's box, the last of the evening, was being bid on.

Evidently the remaining group of hungry men had been spurred to new heights both by Shorty's high bid and the realization that Lorelei and the last box must go together. Pockets were being turned out, money hastily counted, and enthusiasm was at a fever pitch.

"A dollar seventy-five." Apparently the bidding had been going on for some time before I had come out of my stupor.

"Two fifty." Jeff spoke clearly.

"Two seventy-five." I looked at Jeff, tall and remote across the room. He had stopped at two fifty before. Would he do it again?

"Two eighty." To my relief, the voice was not Jeff's. The momentum of the bidding was slowing down.

The auctioneer scanned the men as if to draw out any more prospective buyers.

"How about two ninety?" he called. "Do I hear two ninety?"

"Three dollars and fifty cents." Every head swiveled to see from whom the bid had come, but I didn't need to look. I knew that voice well enough.

I watched Jeff pay for his supper after the auctioneer's gavel had descended for the last time. Lorelei stood and swept toward him, grace and elegance in every line of her bearing. I could picture her moving the same way down a curving staircase at a lavish ball. She would always be queen of whatever group she chose to rule.

They did make a handsome couple. It wasn't hard to see how any man could lose his heart to Lorelei. I just wished it hadn't been the one man to whom my heart would always belong.

Pull yourself together, I reminded myself. *If you love him, love him enough to let go. Remember?*

"Anything wrong, Miss Judith? You're not feeling sick or anything?" Shorty still beamed triumphantly, but a touch of concern crept into his voice.

I forced a smile, although my face felt as though it would shatter. "I'm sorry, Shorty. I guess I was just woolgathering."

A smile of relief brightened his face still more, and I felt ashamed of myself. I hastened to take two plates from the box and fill one of them with pieces of fried chicken, fluffy mashed potatoes, biscuits, and gravy. I wouldn't have thought Shorty's face could have gotten any brighter, but now he fairly glowed.

I took smaller portions for myself and bowed my head to say grace. Shorty looked at me quizzically for a moment after my amen, then began tucking into the food. He concentrated solely on eating for several minutes, and when he finally stopped to catch his breath, his face wore an expression of pure satisfaction.

"No lady's cooked a supper just for me since my ma died when I was fifteen."

"I'm glad you like it." And to my surprise, I found that I meant it. To keep the conversation going, I added, "That was quite a bid you made."

He grinned, then his face darkened. "I thought for a moment ol' Jeff was going to bid me clear out of the running, but he stopped just in time."

That was an area I didn't care to explore. "Tell me about your mother," I ventured.

I had found the right tactic for keeping the talk away from dangerous subjects. Shorty told story after story about growing up as the son of a sharecropper in Arkansas. His father died when he was ten, and he and his mother barely managed to keep going by taking in laundry and doing odd jobs. When she passed away five years later, he decided to head west.

I felt an unexpected softening toward Shorty. I could understand his feelings on the loss of his parents, and the west had seemed to me, too, the door to a brighter future. The realization that we had so much in common brought me up short, and I looked at him with new eyes. When he wasn't devising practical jokes or begging me to marry him, Shorty could actually be pleasant company.

When he saw the apple pie, he set to with relish, polishing off all but the narrow slice I cut for myself. Remembering

Willie's experience, I hoped Shorty wouldn't fall prey to the same malady.

He leaned back in his chair and sighed blissfully. I returned the empty dishes to the box and wondered what came next. Steeling myself, I glanced covertly at the table where Jeff sat with Lorelei. They were smiling and chatting merrily, and Jeff devoured her little sandwiches with every bit as much enjoyment as Shorty had shown with my meal.

People around us began to stir, clearing away the remains of their suppers and shoving chairs and benches back up against the tables. Evidently the evening was over. I dreaded the long drive home.

I swept the last of the crumbs off the table and brushed them into the box. Shorty looked up at me and said, "You know, I really didn't think it would be like this, me actually getting to eat with you and all. I guess I've been pretty hard to be around. Can we kind of . . . start over, do you think?"

I sighed. "Shorty, I just don't know. Right now, I need some time. But . . . I would like for us to be friends, if that's all right."

"Well," he said, pushing away from the table and helping me with my cloak, "it's better than nothing." He grinned and held out his arm.

The crowd had thinned out by the time we made our way to the door. Outside, Jake had drawn the wagon up. Shorty boosted me easily to the wagon bed and said, "Thanks for tonight."

"Thank you for buying my supper," I managed. "And thank you for being my friend." He nodded and gave me a cheerful wink, then went to mount his horse, which had apparently recovered from its limp.

A wave of weariness and misery engulfed me, and I was grateful to be able to settle myself in a front corner before the others got aboard. I pulled the hood of my cloak up so that it shaded my face.

The rest of the party came out on a wave of Lorelei's prattle. I felt too tired and heartsick to rouse myself to greet them, even when Vera laid a solicitous hand on my shoulder.

Neil joined Shorty on horseback, which left only the four of us and Jake in the wagon.

Once, Lorelei directed a remark to me, but before I could make the effort to reply, Vera intervened.

"She's asleep," she snapped, in the manner of a hen defending her only chick.

"Just keep your voices down and leave her be."

All I remember of the endless ride home was that we seemed to float on a stream of Lorelei's constant chatter. Even when I didn't catch her words, her tone indicated she was immensely pleased with herself.

After what seemed an eternity, we pulled up before the ranch house. Charles had left lamps burning low for us, and I stumbled to my room, glad I didn't have to carry a candle.

I threw the cloak and the lovely blue dress over the back of my chair, flung myself across the bed, and slept.

Chapter 13

The following days went by in a blur. My senses had been numbed by my emotional upheaval, and I was content for the time being to go along in that unfeeling state. I knew that, at some point in the near future, I would have to face the prospect of my future and make plans. But now a sort of protective cocoon enveloped me, and I welcomed it.

Avoiding the other adults on the ranch became an obsession. The children made a good excuse, and I took them on long walks on the pretext of getting in as much exercise as possible before the snow fell.

Lorelei unknowingly aided me by monopolizing as much of Jeff's time as possible. "I guess I'm just not cut out for full-time nursing," she declared. "If I spend too much more time in that stuffy little room, I'll be laid as low as Abby. You don't mind giving me a little break now and then to get fresh air, do you?"

Actually, I didn't. Vera agreed to keep Lizzie and Willie under her watchful eye while I stayed with Abby, so I was able to spend nearly all my time either alone with the children or in the sickroom. Abby slept for a good part of each day, which left me free to brood. I found myself with more time to do this as Lorelei discovered an increasing need for fresh air.

"That woman is acting like she owns the place," reported Vera, setting my lunch tray down in Abby's room with a muffled thump. "She actually had the gall to ask me if she could rearrange some of the furniture in the parlor!"

I knew her words were intended to rouse me to action, but I had tried Vera's philosophy of "stand up and fight" and had been defeated soundly. Right now, all I wanted was to lick my wounds in peace.

Charles came to Abby's door every evening and said he would relieve me for supper, but I always insisted he go instead, grateful for the excuse not to have to face Jeff or watch Lorelei's possessiveness. It was cowardly, I knew, but it was hard to care about that or anything else from within my protective cocoon.

But little by little, small things began to work their way through unsuspected chinks in my carefully constructed armor, fanning to life sparks of feeling I thought would never surface again.

Lizzie and Willie dogged my steps every time I set foot outside their mother's room. They had been models of good behavior ever since the night of the box supper social, and it was evidence of my numbed state of mind that that alone didn't send me flying into a panic.

During one of our long walks, we stopped to rest in the shelter of an enormous cedar. The children arranged themselves on either side of me, each holding one of my hands. We sat like that, listening to the wind stirring the branches, until I felt their small bodies slump against me. I eased them down so their heads could rest in my lap.

Lizzie stirred and reached for my hand again. Taking it, she pressed it against her cheek. A lump formed in my throat. Willie slept contentedly, a soft snore escaping his lips from time to time. Lizzie, however, whimpered repeatedly and squirmed in her sleep, squeezing my hand as though for reassurance.

The lump in my throat grew until it reached the bursting point, and by the time both children's eyelids flickered open, slow tears were coursing down my cheeks. Uncharacteristically, they didn't say a word all the way back to the house.

I left them with Vera and fled to the sanctuary of Abby's room, thrusting an astonished Lorelei out into the hallway. I sat straight in the bedside chair, lips pressed together, hands clasped in my lap, feet arranged just so, as if by holding my body in rigid alignment, I could calm the tumult that raged within.

"Abby," I whispered to the sleeping form through lips all too inclined to tremble, "I wish you could hear me. I thought things would be so different by now. I'm so confused. Jeff and Lorelei are together all the time now, and ever since the social, he's seemed like a total stranger.

"Right up until that night, I felt sure there was something wonderful between us, but I guess I was wrong. Maybe he never really did get over Lorelei, after all. I turned it over to the Lord because I . . . I love Jeff and I want him to be happy. I thought that would solve everything — but then, why am I so miserable?"

I put my face in my hands and wept, trying to stifle the sound so Abby wouldn't be disturbed. If only she were well again! I needed her counsel and friendship now more than ever.

A gentle touch on my knee made me bring my head upright with a start. To my surprise, I found myself staring into Abby's calm gray eyes.

"What is it?" she asked gently.

"Oh, Abby!" I cried. "I didn't mean to wake you."

"Why are you crying, dear? Can I help?"

"It's . . . it's not important," I answered, trying to keep my voice level. Much as I longed to share everything with her, the burden of my problems was the last thing she needed to bear.

"But, Mama, dear, you seemed worried over something."

I stared uncomprehendingly as the impact of her words sank into my consciousness.

"Mama?" I repeated blankly.

"Is it about Charles? I know you think I'm making the wrong choice in marrying him, but I love him, Mama, truly I do. And I know he'll make a kind and wonderful husband."

The gray eyes held mine steadily, but there was no doubt that the face she saw was from another place and time.

I drew the covers up over her gently, patted her hand, and murmured sounds meant to be comforting. I withdrew from the room, closed the door softly, and bolted down the hall in search of Charles, Jeff, Vera, anyone who could dispel this nightmare. My own troubles were, for the moment, firmly thrust aside.

Worried days and wakeful nights followed each other in a seemingly endless procession. Abby went from delirium to lucidity and back again while we all performed what tasks we could for her comfort and chafed at our helplessness to do anything of significance.

Vera, Lorelei, and I took turns watching at her bedside during the day, while Charles took the night watches. Consequently, Jeff shouldered full responsibility for the ranch. He was away from the house all day, except for supper, the one time we all gathered for a meal.

I alternated between helping Vera in the kitchen and minding the children when I was not on duty in the sickroom.

"What do you think?" Vera asked me as we peeled potatoes one morning.

"About Abby?" I asked.

She nodded, her brow furrowed with worry. "I thought she looked like she'd gained a little this morning, didn't you?"

"I honestly don't know what to think," I

replied cautiously. "Sometimes she seems as if she's almost back to normal. Then she starts talking like she's a girl in Virginia again."

"I know." Vera sighed. "I'm so afraid for Charles and those little ones." She paused in her work to wipe the back of her hand across one cheek.

"Isn't there anything we can do? There must be something! It's unbearable to sit by and watch her waste away like this."

Vera shook her head wearily. "There's not a thing more that any of us can do . . . except pray."

"I've been praying for her almost constantly. We all have."

"Then I guess we'll just have to leave it in His hands, won't we?"

I nodded. A feeling that a turning point must soon be reached pervaded the house, and the resulting tension spread over us like a pall.

Everyone felt the strain, but I ached especially for the children, who were denied even the satisfaction of performing little duties for their mother. Charles had ordered that they be allowed in the sickroom only when Abby was asleep. I knew they missed her company but had to agree they needed to be protected from the shock of realizing their own mother didn't always recognize them.

The nightly gathering at the supper table was primarily for their benefit, to preserve a sense of normalcy, but it served to give the rest of us an anchor as well. I resumed eating with the family, finding that the sense of unity gave us all added strength.

It was at the dinner table one evening that Jeff shared a piece of astonishing news. "I had a long visit with the Reverend Carver today," he said, helping himself to slices of roast beef.

I winced and fastened my eyes on my plate. I hadn't seen the pastor since the day of his proposal, nor did I care to.

"And what did the good reverend have to say?" asked Charles, with a sarcasm I knew would not have been present if not for his anxiety.

Jeff took a moment to swallow his food. "I think I've discovered the reason his sermons have seemed so far off the mark. The man doesn't know the Christ he preaches."

I stared at Jeff in spite of myself.

"Do you mean he's here under false pretenses?" asked Charles. "He isn't even a Christian?"

"I should have said he *didn't* know

Christ," Jeff replied. "He met the Lord this afternoon."

"I don't understand," put in Lorelei. "How could he be a minister and not be a Christian?"

Jeff looked at her thoughtfully before replying. "I had business in town this morning," he said, "and as I was about to head back home, I bumped into him on the street. He asked me about Abby, and I told him she wasn't doing well at all."

"As he'd know if he ever bothered to call out here." Charles snorted in disgust.

"Yes, we touched on that topic," Jeff said with a crooked grin. "I told him it was hard to see her this way, that if it weren't for knowing the Lord, it would be more than any of us could stand.

"And do you know what he did?" He shook his head, remembering. "He coughed and spluttered and said, 'Yes, I'm sure Mrs. Bradley has led an exemplary life. And if her days should be drawing to a close, her works will precede her and open the way to paradise.' "

"He actually said *that?*" I gasped. Jeff didn't even glance in my direction.

"He did. So I sat him down in front of the store and asked him just exactly what he did believe."

"I'll bet it has something to do with 'the inherent goodness of man,'" Charles quipped.

"That and a lot besides," Jeff said. "It seems his grandfather and two uncles are ministers at churches back east. When it came time for him to decide on his life's work, he just figured he'd follow in the family tradition."

"And what's wrong with that?" Lorelei challenged. "It's a noble and respectable calling."

"Yes," Jeff answered slowly, "if it's the Lord who does the calling. But Carver never saw it that way. He just looked on it as a job like any other.

"Apparently he got in with some progressive-thinking church that thought his brand of religion was fine. Then when his health failed, he decided he'd spread the light of all his knowledge to the poor, backward souls in the west while he recuperated. He never could understand why he got such a cool reception here."

"Until today?" Charles prompted.

"That's right. We took a long walk through the Bible he was carrying, and he found out that man has no inherent goodness and our works don't mean a thing if they're not based on faith in Jesus Christ as Savior and Lord."

"You mean he was converted right then and there?"

"Right where we sat. Once he got past the idea that he was able to make himself good enough for heaven, he asked me, 'Then how can I be saved?' Just like the Philippian jailer," he chuckled.

"It was wonderful to see. He bowed his head and repented and asked the Lord to save him. He's a new man in Christ!"

"That is wonderful," Charles agreed. "Will he stay on and preach, then?"

"No." Jeff shook his head. "He said he thought he'd spend some time in study to see what he really is supposed to be saying. I think that in time the Lord will have a fine spokesman in him."

"What does 'repent' mean?" Lizzie asked. I jumped a little. The children had been so quiet through supper that I had almost forgotten their presence.

"What does it mean?" she repeated, wide-eyed.

"Well, honey," said Charles, "it's kind of like when a man realizes he's been going down the wrong trail and he needs to turn around and go the right way. It's when you decide to turn back from going your own way and go God's way instead. Understand?" She nodded, and Charles rose from his seat and gave her a warm hug.

We all prepared to go our separate ways — Charles to sit with Abby, Jeff to a final check of the ranch for the night, me to see the children to bed, and Lorelei to her beauty sleep. I dipped a corner of Willie's napkin in his water tumbler and was using it to scrub his face when I heard a cry behind me. Lizzie had laid her head down on the white tablecloth and was sobbing wildly.

Charles and Lorelei had already gone. Jeff looked at me with as much astonishment as I felt.

"What is it, Lizzie?" I asked, giving Willie's cheek a final rub.

Her sobs turned to wails and I hurried to quiet her.

"I . . . I . . . I repent!" she choked out.

"Of what, honey?" I stroked her hair.

"I lied to Uncle Jeff, and I knew it was wrong, and I want to repent!"

"Lied to me?" Jeff knelt beside her, eyes full of concern. "What about?"

Lizzie sat up, her face swollen and tear streaked. I handed her one of the napkins, and she blew her nose thoroughly. Her breath came in quick little gasps, and she turned to her uncle.

"It was the day of the box supper social," she gulped. "Remember when you asked Willie and me to find out what Judith's box looked like so you could bid on it?"

Jeff nodded. I stirred uneasily, thinking this was a line of thought neither of us wished to pursue.

"I remember." His voice betrayed nothing.

"And remember I told you she said her box and her dress would match?"

I drew a quick breath, remembering my blue dress and Lorelei's blue box.

He nodded solemnly.

"Well —" she faltered, "I lied. I knew her box was the green one with the pretty flowers."

Jeff glanced up at me. Our eyes met and held, but neither of us spoke.

He looked Lizzie squarely in the eye. "Then why? Why tell me something that wasn't true?"

Her shoulders shook as the sobs took hold of her again. "I thought it would be funny," she said. "A good joke. But it wasn't funny at all. I never thought about you getting that old Lorelei's box by mistake, and now she says she's going to marry you, and Mama's so sick, and, oh, Uncle Jeff, everything's going wrong!"

She threw her arms around his neck, and he held her close. "It's all right," he said, rocking her in his arms. "Everybody does wrong sometimes. But now you've told me about it, and I forgive you. So it's over. You don't need to worry about it anymore."

Instead of being soothed by this, Lizzie's agitation increased, and she clung to him all the more tightly. "But I want to be clean," she wailed. "I want to be all new, like the Reverend Carver."

A joyful smile broke out on Jeff's face. "Well, Lizzie," he said, "that's a real easy thing to arrange. Let's go find your father." And he carried her out of the room in search of Charles.

I let out a pent-up sigh of relief. It looked as though two new children would enter the Kingdom of God that day. I turned to the wide-eyed Willie and herded him off to bed.

I lay awake for a long time, thinking over Lizzie's confession. How different things would be right now if she had not unwittingly fabricated a story that would play right into Lorelei's hands!

Or would they? I wondered.

On the one hand, Jeff had not denied Lizzie's statement that he intended to buy my box at the social. I had not, then, been mistaken about the warmth of his manner toward me on the way to town that night.

But, I reflected, there had been opportunity since then to explain the mix-up if he wanted to. Had the mistake turned out to be a favorable one for him, rekindling his feelings for Lorelei? If what Lizzie quoted Lorelei as saying was true, it would certainly seem that the social acted as the catalyst that brought them back together.

I tossed and turned, pummeling my pillow into a myriad of shapes as I examined the pieces of this puzzle and tried to fit them into a meaningful pattern. Finally admitting defeat, I breathed, "Lord, it's all Yours. I can't begin to understand what's happened," and promptly fell asleep.

Chapter 14

I awoke well before daybreak, feeling fully rested and ready for action. No matter how hard I tried, I could not go back to sleep, nor could I convince myself to burrow under the covers against the chill morning air.

I dressed quickly and crept down the hall to the kitchen. Even Vera wasn't up and about yet. I pulled one of her shawls from a peg near the door and stepped outside.

If I hadn't been fully awake, it would have taken only that first moment of contact with the frosty air to make me so. Even the warm shawl couldn't stop the icy fingers from raising gooseflesh along my arms.

I paced up and down the porch and filled my lungs with the invigorating air. A light frost crunched beneath my feet, and I reveled in having this moment to myself.

The indigo hue of the sky was fading to

gray. One by one, the stars were lost to sight. It was impossible, I felt, to witness all this beauty without being aware of the One who made it. I brought my concerns to Him one by one: Abby's failing health; Lizzie and her new life in Christ; Jeff, Lorelei, and their engagement; and direction for my own future. In this time alone with God, even that uncertainty paled in significance.

Back inside, I had biscuits mixed and in the oven by the time Vera walked in. "Well, aren't you bright-eyed this morning!" she said, blinking in surprise.

I smiled at her. "I couldn't sleep. I've been getting some things straightened out between me and the Lord."

"Good for you." She squeezed my shoulders. "I've been worried about you."

"I'm sorry. I guess I've been feeling so sorry for myself that I didn't think how my attitude might affect anyone else. It won't happen again. We all have enough to worry about without my adding to it."

"Well, it's over now." She eyed me critically. "You're feeling a lot better, aren't you?"

"I feel fine," I said, laughing. "Ready for anything." And it was a good thing, because Vera kept me flying from one task to another until well after lunchtime.

We were standing on the porch, taking a few moments to catch our breath, when Neil rode up.

"I had to go into town yesterday. They were holding a bunch of mail. It was late when I got back, so I held on to it till today." He tossed a bundle of envelopes to Vera and loped away.

Vera glanced through the envelopes quickly, then went back to examine each one more thoroughly. She pulled one, grimier than the rest, from the pile. "Miss Judith Alder," she read, holding it gingerly by one corner. "Looks like the dogs delivered this one." She handed it to me, and I accepted it with quickening breath.

A glance at the handwriting verified that it was from Uncle Matthew. No one else I knew used quite the same slapdash scrawl.

I stared at the missive. There was something awe inspiring about receiving word from him only a few hours after praying for guidance.

The confusing whirl of thoughts from the night before renewed their dance through my mind. Jeff had been ready to buy my box. So, buying Lorelei's instead hadn't really been his intention. He had to dance attendance on her that evening, but certainly no one had forced him to do so since. All he had to do was say the word, and I would be willing to stay forever. Abby said he was through with Lorelei. But Lorelei said . . .

Impatiently, I wedged my finger under the flap and ripped the envelope open. I was only indulging in idle speculation. I had prayed for direction; was I willing to accept it?

"Would you look at this!" Vera exclaimed. "Charles! *Charles!*"

"What is it?" I asked, glad of the interruption.

"What is it?" Charles echoed, striding onto the porch, followed by Jeff.

"Look at the return address." Vera waved the envelope under his nose. "Isn't that the name of one of the doctors who came through last spring?"

Charles had to grab it from her to hold it still enough to read the name. "I think so," he agreed. "Jeff, come take a look at this."

As the two men moved farther down the length of the porch, I pulled my own letter from its envelope and read:

Dear Niece,

There have been a few problems with creditors since the trading post burned down. I have decided I'd be healthier in a different climate. By the time you get this, I'll be headed for greener pastures. Your aunt always said I was a shiftless no-account, and I guess maybe she was right. You'll be better off staying where you are or going back to Missouri.

Your affectionate uncle,
Matthew

I stared at the paper, willing it to say more. Was this the divine guidance I sought? All it did was close one door and leave me as much in the dark as before. Stay or go back east — those were my choices. My heart was here. But was there a reason to stay? The reason I hoped for?

"Praise the Lord." I looked up at the sound of Charles's voice. He and Jeff stood grinning at each other. "Praise the Lord!" he repeated, and the brothers slapped each other on the back.

"Well, are you going to share it with Judith and me," Vera snapped, "or are we going to have to take that letter from you and read it ourselves?"

Charles looked from one of us to the other as though he didn't know where to begin. Jeff clapped him on the shoulder and laughed. "You'd better tell them before they come after you."

His brother grinned and shook his head as if to clear it. "You're right, Vera. This is from Dr. Anderson. He was out in this area last spring," he explained to me, "and examined Abby while he was here. He was just as puzzled as anyone and had no idea what could be causing her illness.

"However, he writes that on returning to Boston, he has learned that promising work is being done with patients who have symptoms similar to Abby's. He believes if we take her back east, there is every hope she'll recover."

This time I was able to add my heartfelt praise to the others'. To think that after all, Charles and the children might not lose Abby! Truly, this was a day of answered prayer.

"When will you start?" Vera demanded.

"Just as soon as possible," said Charles. "This week, if we can. Even though her mind wanders, it seems to me she's rallied physically the past few days. I want to do it soon, before she loses any more ground. There's no point in starting for Boston if she can't stand the trip."

"What about the children?"

"I think they should come with us.

Abby's mother would be glad to take care of them, I'm sure. Jeff will have to run the place alone, and he'll be busy enough without having to watch out for them."

Jeff chuckled. "You sound as though you've been planning this for weeks instead of five minutes."

Charles smiled. "The Lord must have been laying the groundwork for this in my mind all along. The ideas just seem to be falling into place." He stopped abruptly. "Except for one thing." He looked at me intently.

"Judith, I know it's presumptuous of me to ask this of you, and I wouldn't except for Abby's sake. I know how much it means to you to be able to join your uncle. But we'll need someone to care for the children on the trip back. Could you possibly consider postponing your plans long enough to help us?"

Uncle Matthew's letter seemed to burn in my hand. Little did they know how my options had narrowed. I thought rapidly. If Abby and Charles were going to leave, I could hardly remain here. Unless . . . I looked at Jeff, hoping he would step forward and give me a reason to stay.

He didn't make a move.

This was, then, evidently the guidance I

had looked for, though hardly in the form I had hoped. I looked at Charles, squared my shoulders, and said, "Of course I'll go."

The days of preparation flew by as the details for the trip were worked out. Vera and I starched, ironed, and packed clothes for the five of us who would be traveling, took turns tending to Abby, and tried to maintain some semblance of control over Lizzie and Willie, who were wild with excitement at the prospect of the journey.

Charles ran himself ragged trying to get all the travel plans in order before Abby's slight increase in strength waned. We would go by wagon to Raton, where we would rest overnight before taking the eastbound stagecoach to Dodge and the train to Boston.

He wired Abby's mother, who replied that, rather than having the children stay with her, she would take rooms in Boston. That way she could be near her daughter, and the children wouldn't have to be separated from their parents.

And Jeff — Jeff worked as though driven, trying to live up to the responsibility placed upon him, consulting with Charles to be sure they were in agreement over what should be done during the coming winter. If our time together had been scarce before, it was all but nonexistent now. We didn't exchange more than a few words during the days of preparation.

I told myself it was just as well. There was nothing left to say.

I, too, pushed myself to the limit through the long days of activity, trying to stay busy enough to ignore the growing sense of loneliness. Not since the Parkers slipped away and left me on the prairie had I felt so utterly alone. The fact that I was in the midst of people only made the emptiness more difficult to bear.

I knew well that once we arrived in Boston, with Abby's mother at hand to care for the children, my usefulness would be at an end. They would all expect me to make my way back and join Uncle Matthew.

Charles generously insisted on paying my way back to New Mexico, and I hadn't been able to bring myself to tell him, or anyone, that I was even more adrift now than when I first climbed out of the chuck wagon at their doorstep.

I knew the Bradleys well enough by now to realize that if they had any inkling of my true situation, they would feel obligated to help me. I could no longer presume on such generosity when I could in no way repay them.

"Fight for what you want," Vera had advised. I fought, in the only ways I knew how, and had come out the loser. I was completely at loose ends, totally dependent upon the Lord to show me the next step to take.

In due time, I supposed, I would get over Uncle Matthew's betrayal and be able to look back on my months in New Mexico as a lovely interlude, a memory to be treasured through the remainder of my life. I wondered dully if time would also heal the aching void I felt when I thought of leaving Jeff forever.

One day, in the midst of all the preparations, Vera and I were folding clothes and arranging them in a trunk with Lorelei's indifferent help. After Vera had to refold a third dress Lorelei had carelessly wadded, she told her to sit on the bed and watch.

Lorelei moved instead to the mirror and occupied herself with twisting already perfect ringlets into shape around her lovely face.

I was smoothing the folds of the sky blue dress I had worn to the box supper social when Charles looked in through the open door.

"Everything going all right?" We assured him it was. His gaze lingered on the dress in my hands and grew wistful. "I'm glad you're taking that dress, Judith. Abby would want you to consider all the clothes she gave you as yours to keep."

"I'm not taking this for myself," I told him. "This is for Abby to wear when she's well." His eyes misted over, and he turned abruptly and left.

"Do you know," said Lorelei, still primping, "I believe I'll travel back with you all. All this nursing has just about worn me out, and I think I need a change."

I stared at her, dumbfounded. "But what about the wedding?"

"Oh, that," she murmured vaguely and swept out of the room.

"Well, forevermore!" Vera exclaimed. "What on earth's gotten into her?"

I had no answer for her. The question in my mind was how Jeff would feel, being turned down twice by the same woman.

Somehow we all managed to complete our assigned tasks, and the day of departure came. I hurried outside at dawn to have a few minutes to myself. My eyes swept across the landscape, taking in the shrubs and trees close at hand as they emerged from the dark folds of night and moving on to the vast reaches of prairie that swept out to the horizon.

I felt a part of this land. It was home to me in a way that the once-familiar streets of St. Joseph never had been. It drew me now, and I stepped back almost involuntarily, as if to break the spell.

"Good-bye," I whispered, knowing a part of me would always remain here.

Saying good-bye to Vera was nearly impossible. Poor Vera! She had taken care of Charles, Abby, and the children for so long, she felt as if part of her was being physically torn out to see them go. If she had her way, she would have gone all the way to Boston to be sure her charges were properly cared for. But Charles convinced her she needed to stay and keep house for Jeff.

I waited until she finished tucking Abby in and making sure that she had done everything possible for her comfort. She stood back from the buggy, biting her lower lip and blinking rapidly.

Finally the last piece of luggage had been loaded, and we were ready to go. Charles had hired a buggy for Abby to ride in to Raton, and he was to ride with her, with Jeff driving them. Lorelei, somewhat miffed at being left out of the more comfortable arrangements, was seated next to the driver of the wagon carrying our luggage. Lizzie and Willie waited for me in a second wagon.

I turned to Vera, trying for her sake to keep the parting on a steady note. "Good-bye," I said. "You'll never know how much your friendship has meant to me. I'll never forget you." I heard my voice climbing higher, nearly breaking, and it proved Vera's undoing.

Her face working, she drew me into her arms and we clung to each other, letting the tears flow. Then we stood facing each other, mopping our cheeks with sodden handkerchiefs, and Vera tried to speak, but the words would not come. No matter. I knew how she felt and knew that her friendship and respect were things to be valued highly.

I sat between Lizzie and Willie, and we waved until the house and Vera were out of sight. "Thus ends the pioneer life of Judith Alder," I murmured.

The nip in the air made the horses lively and anxious to be moving, but even so, the ride into Raton lasted the whole day. Charles hurried into the hotel to secure rooms for all of us, and I helped him settle Abby for the night after he carried her up-stairs. The long drive had not fatigued her as much as we feared, and I prayed her stamina would hold throughout the trip.

We gathered in the dining room adjacent to the hotel lobby. The food was well prepared and plentiful, and it was a relief not to have to cook and help clean up after the meal.

Tired as we were, no one spoke much except Lorelei, who managed to find something to criticize about her room, the food, and the service. When Lizzie and Willie all but fell asleep at their places, I used the excuse to take them upstairs and put them to bed in the room we shared. Lorelei's constant faultfinding was more than I could bear just then.

Chapter 15

Once again I rose before the sun. Dressing quietly in the dark, I managed to slip out without waking the children. The stage did not leave until midmorning, and I wanted to come to terms with myself on my last morning in New Mexico Territory before I had to face the others.

I dared not go too far away in case someone should need me, but I walked softly along the boardwalk until I was several buildings away from the hotel and stood facing the east, awaiting the sunrise.

So much had happened; so many changes had taken place. I was not the same person I had been when I left Missouri.

I could just make out the building across the street. The telegraph office. I wondered if I should wire Aunt Phoebe when it opened to let her know I would be returning soon.

Everything within me rebelled at the

thought. Even though I was no longer the same person, I was limited in what I could do on my own. I wondered idly what positions might be available in Boston for a Christian young lady of moderate education and no experience.

"Good morning."

I gasped and whirled, a hand at my throat. So engrossed had I been in my thoughts that I hadn't heard Jeff approach.

"G–good morning," I faltered, fighting for composure.

He looked down at me through the graying light. "I didn't mean to frighten you," he said gently.

Caught off guard like that, I couldn't think of a thing to say. The lines around his eyes were more deeply etched than before, and his face looked thinner. I thought angrily of how much damage Lorelei had done and with what little feeling.

I longed to trace the contours of his face with my fingertips. Instead, I laced my fingers tightly together so they would not betray me of their own accord and turned away slightly, feigning interest in the telegraph office across the street.

"Planning to send a wire?"

I shook my head yes, then no, then shrugged. "I don't know. I thought I might let my aunt know that I'd be coming back soon." The prospect seemed no less dismal when voiced aloud. I placed my hands around a post and held on for support.

"I guess you'll be glad to get back to your family and civilization again."

Splinters from the post bit into my fingers as I gripped it to keep from crying out that what I wanted was to stay with him, wherever he might be.

He didn't seem to notice my lack of response. "Seems like the people you care about the most always leave," he said in a low voice.

"Maybe they don't always want to." It was out before I could stop myself.

"You mean Lorelei?"

"I wasn't talking about —" I wheeled to face him. "What do you mean?"

"I mean," he said slowly, "that Lorelei wasn't any too happy when I sent her away."

I must have been even more tired than I thought. Nothing was making sense this morning. "You sent Lorelei away?"

He nodded. "I told her we found out long ago we weren't meant for each other. No use raking up dead coals. She didn't take it well. I think she's been used to being the one who's called it quits."

I thought back over the last few days. "Then that's why she's acted so strangely lately." A thought was trying to penetrate my fog-enshrouded brain, but I couldn't quite grasp it.

Jeff seemed to be having the same difficulty. "If you weren't talking about Lorelei . . . what did you mean?" I started to turn away again, but he placed one hand on each shoulder and looked squarely into my eyes. "What did you mean?" he repeated.

"I just meant that . . . that people who leave don't always go because they want to." My voice shook. I wasn't saying it well at all.

He wet his lips and spoke carefully, as if searching for the right words. "Do you mean, Judith, that you don't want to go?" I nodded mutely. "Then why — ?"

"What choice do I have? Uncle Matthew wrote that he couldn't take me, and I couldn't very well stay on at the ranch with Charles and Abby gone. And I thought that, well, you and Lorelei . . . I mean, I didn't think there was a reason for me to stay."

The next thing I knew, his arms were around me, holding me close. One hand pressed my head tight against his chest.

His breath stirred my hair as he whispered, "To think I was almost fool enough to let you get away!"

I drew back a little, still remaining within the circle of his arms. The lines in his face had disappeared, and he looked boyishly exuberant. I found my arms wrapped around him, clinging as though they would never let him go.

His work-hardened hand caressed my cheek. "It's been tearing me apart to think of you leaving, but I know how hard life can be out here. I didn't want to take you away from the comforts you'd known, when I had so little to offer."

"Little!" Tears stung my eyes. "Everything I'd ever want is right here." I searched his face. "You're sure?" I asked, and his response was more than enough to convince me.

The dawn broke then, bathing us in a golden haze. Joy welled up inside me and bubbled over into a spring of delight. Let Uncle Matthew and others like him search for hidden riches. It was enough for me to have the treasure of Jeff's love.

"We'll have to make some plans," he whispered.

"Plans?" I repeated dreamily. Then awareness jolted me back to reality. "Why,

I suppose — Jeff! What about Abby? What about the children? What about — ?"

He stopped the flow of words effectively with a kiss that left me breathless. "What did you have in mind?" I asked meekly.

"I suggest," he said, tucking my hand into the crook of his arm and escorting me back toward the hotel, "I send word to the ranch that I won't be back for a while. Jake and Shorty can hold the fort for a couple of weeks.

"Then I can ride along with you on the train as far as, oh, say Missouri. If you like, we can go ahead and wire your aunt from here and ask if she'd like to attend the wedding.

"And then," he said, cupping my cheek in his hand, "we'll travel back to the ranch — back to our home — on our honeymoon."

I sighed in blissful contentment. Once again, though, duty reared its stern head. "But what about the children?"

One corner of his mouth turned up in a crooked grin. "We'll let Charles put Lorelei in charge of them. It will be a good experience for her."

I turned back to face the sunrise. The golden glow gave way to a rosy hue. It was a new dawn, a new day.

A new beginning.

Carol Cox

Carol makes her home in northern Arizona. She and her pastor husband minister in two churches, so boredom is never a problem. Family activities with her husband, college-age son, and young daughter also keep her busy, but she still manages to find time to write. She considers writing a joy and a calling. Since her first book was published in 1998, she has seven novels and nine novellas to her credit, with more currently in progress. Fiction has always been her first love. Fascinated by the history of the Southwest, she has traveled extensively throughout the region and uses it as the setting for many of her stories. Carol loves to hear from her readers! You can send E-mail to her at: carolcoxbooks@yahoo.com.

The employees of Thorndike Press hope you have enjoyed this Large Print book. All our Thorndike and Wheeler Large Print titles are designed for easy reading, and all our books are made to last. Other Thorndike Press Large Print books are available at your library, through selected bookstores, or directly from us.

For information about titles, please call:

(800) 223-1244

or visit our Web site at:

www.gale.com/thorndike
www.gale.com/wheeler

To share your comments, please write:

Publisher
Thorndike Press
295 Kennedy Memorial Drive
Waterville, ME 04901